KU-632-549

LEM   W   GAY

HOT SPUR

Greed, lust for power and ruthless ambition are what drive Richard Grant, and all he needs is the Big G to consolidate his hold on the territory. Only his cousin Harry, the legitimate heir, stands in his way. When Harry guns down the hired killers sent on Richard's orders, a crooked sheriff and judge make sure he goes to prison. On his release he faces more assassins sent to make sure he never makes his rightful claim. Harry has no choice but to go gunning for his cousin at the Hot Spur saloon, and only one of them will be left standing.

HOT SPUR

NORFOLK LIBRARY AND
INFORMATION SERVICE

SUPPLIER

INVOICE No.

ORDER DATE

HOT SPUR

by

Elliot James

Dales Large Print Books
Long Preston, North Yorkshire,
BD23 4ND, England.

British Library Cataloguing in Publication Data.

James, Elliot
    Hot spur.

A catalogue record of this book is
available from the British Library

    ISBN   978-1-84262-504-0 pbk

NORFOLK LIBRARY AND
INFORMATION SERVICE

SUPPLIER	MAGNA
INVOICE No.	IO47665
ORDER DATE	25-2-11
COPY No.	

First published in Great Britain in 2006 by Robert Hale Ltd.

Copyright © Elliot James 2006

Cover illustration © Koenig by arrangement with
Norma Editorial S.A.

The right of Elliot James to be identified as the author of this
work has been asserted by him in accordance with the
Copyright, Designs and Patents Act, 1988

Published in Large Print 2007 by arrangement with
Robert Hale Limited

All Rights reserved. No part of this publication may be
reproduced, stored in a retrieval system, or transmitted in any
form or by any means, electronic, mechanical, photocopying,
recording or otherwise without the prior permission of the
Copyright owner.

Dales Large Print is an imprint of Library Magna Books Ltd.

Printed and bound in Great Britain by
T.J. (International) Ltd., Cornwall, PL28 8RW

1

Tom Grant stood on the porch of the hotel, lit a cigar and contemplated what he would do to entertain himself. Dusk had settled and a sprinkling of lights was bringing life to the main street. He could hear the piano tinkling from Big Bessie's bar. For a moment he stood in the quiet of the hotel porch and puffed contentedly on his cigar. He was wondering whether he should go on down to Bessie's and take a girl to one of the rooms upstairs.

'Goddamn it, I must be getting old if'n I have to decide to have a whore or not,' he mused.

Time was Tom would have spruced himself up, sashayed down to the nearest saloon, had a few drinks and finished up the night with a woman.

He never told his wife, Dorothy about these adventures.

'Usually I have a few quiet drinks and mebby a game of cards – nothing too heavy,' he told her once. 'And then amble on back to the hotel and bed. There ain't much else to do in a cow town 'nless you wanna go down the whorehouse and that ain't for me.'

Unbeknownst to him she could smell the cheap perfume that still lingered on his clothes even after the trek back home, but she never let on.

He stepped out onto the sidewalk and ambled towards the saloon, the piano drawing him irresistibly with its seductive siren song. Tuba's nightlife was beginning to stir.

Tuba was a largish cow town on the margin of the trail drives that pointed north to the cattle yards which held beef for the big cities. It owed its prosperity to this very fact. Trail drivers needed a stopover to replenish their reserves. Tuba had plenty of good grass in the vicinity and an abundant supply of water from the Scoop, a long, shallow, lazy river that coiled around the town like a lariat. The trail herds could stop to graze and put back a little weight before the final push north.

On top of these facilities was another benefit. The area abounded with enterprising cattlemen willing to do a deal with the herd bosses, thus saving on the time and energy to drive the cattle the final leg north.

The money might be less than the expected sale price in the stockyards but, weighed against everything else, sometimes it seemed right to take the money, get back to the ranches and let someone else take responsibility for the herd. Tom Grant had just completed such a deal.

Tom was a slim man nudging towards his sixtieth year. Beneath his Stetson his hair was white and a large white moustache drooped from beneath his nostrils. His face was lean and his skin was bronzed from spending long hours outdoors, riding herd on the prime steers he raised back home. Right now he reckoned he deserved an evening of relaxation after hard days of trail herding.

Later that night Tom Grant rolled off his five-dollar whore and lay back contentedly. All the time he had sweated on top of the plump woman she had groaned and writhed beneath him reassuring him he was the best thing that had happened to her in a long time. When he made no effort to leave she turned to him.

'Are you finished, cowboy?'

He blinked at her foolishly. 'Why, sure I'm finished.'

'OK Grandad. Thanks for the good time. I

gotta git some more business while the night's still young.'

It was a few moments before he realized what she meant.

'Huh, yeah, sure I guess,' he muttered foolishly.

Grandad! He rolled from the bed as she turned up the lamp. Grandad! As he struggled into his clothes he kept glancing surreptitiously at the woman. Hell, she was no chicken herself. Hard to tell her age with all that paint and powder over her face. All his content was gone as he stumped down the stairs to the barroom.

Even at this late hour the room was still crowded with men drinking and talking loudly as men do after a convivial evening. Some of the card-tables were busy.

Tom shouldered up to the bar and ordered whiskey. He liked beer to chase his whiskey but as he grew older he found his capacity to hold large quantities of liquid in his bladder had diminished.

When he left Big Bessie's the place was still crowded with those men with enough money to keep on drinking. There seemed to be a steady traffic to and from the rooms upstairs as the whores worked the drunken crowd.

Trying to keep a steady walk back along the boardwalk towards the hotel, Tom was still sore at the woman.

'Grandad,' he muttered indignantly. 'I can keep up with the best of them in a whorehouse. She warn't no chicken herself. Well past fifty if'n she were a day.'

A shadowy figure was coming towards him on the sidewalk. As they drew level the man held up a rolled cigarette.

'Howdy, friend. Got a light?'

'Light, sure,' Tom answered as he fumbled in his vest pocket for a sulphur head. He heard a sound behind him on the boardwalk but took no notice as he grunted with satisfaction.

'Here ya're, friend.'

An arm surrounded his neck and he was pulled backwards.

'What the hell...!'

The man in front drove a fist into his stomach. The wind was punched from Tom. But Tom was a tough old coot. He had been in many a barroom brawl and knew a few tricks. His boot lashed out and caught his assailant in the knee. The man grunted and backed off. Tom flung his head back and felt a satisfying crunch as his skull connected with something soft.

'You old bastard!'

'Git him down here for Christ's sake!'

Tom let himself go limp and the man holding him struggled to hold on to him. When Tom straightened up abruptly the top of his head connected with the man's chin. They both went down as Tom backpedalled rapidly.

The grip on his neck loosened and Tom rolled to one side. Something hard crashed into the back of the old man's head. Lights exploded in his brain and he collapsed face down on the wooden sidewalk.

The pain in his head was intolerable. He groaned and could resist only feebly as he was dragged off the street and down into the alley.

'The old bastard – he about broke my jaw with his head.'

'Finish him quick an' take what we can find. It has to look like robbery.'

'Yeah, but I'd rather make it real slow. My face feels like it's bin in a meat-grinder.'

Tom was swimming in and out of consciousness. He was lying on his face in the alley. Somehow he could not get his limbs to work. The pain in his head was the worst he could ever remember. He felt an awful sickness in his guts. The men's voices droned in his head but he could make no sense of what they said.

Something crashed on to the top of his head. He gasped and gagged. His skull collapsed on the third or fourth blow. He twitched and went limp and could feel no more blows as the top of his head was reduced to pulp.

2

Tom Grant's widow Dorothy drove her buggy up to the ranch house of the Big G. Since Tom's murder she had become a regular visitor to the ranch to visit her dead husband's brother.

No progress had been made in tracking down her husband's killers. It was this matter Dorothy had come to discuss with her brother-in-law.

'I've received a reply to the letter I had written to the authorities in Tuba,' her brother-in-law told her. 'They agree that Tom's death was unfortunate and extend their sympathies. However they add no more than what we already know – that Tom was slain by persons unknown. As far as they can ascertain the motive was robbery. They state they are doing all they can to catch the perpetrators of the crime. I don't know what else we can do.'

'Brother, what has happened to the fire in your soul? That was your blood-brother murdered in Detroit. You and he were from the same rootstock. You and he worked hard to build the name of Grant into a respected force within the county. Think you not to look closer into this filthy murder?

'Look at me, brother! Tell me! Who benefits from Tom's death? Who was named as his executor?'

Under the scrutiny of his sister-in-law John Grant stirred uneasily in his chair but did not answer her query. Instead he tried to distract her.

'Care you for a little refreshment, sister?'

'Yes, the refreshment I need is justice. I want justice and revenge for the untimely death of my husband. Tom did not deserve this. He was looking forward to a peaceful retirement. Think on it, man. What if it were you lying in the morgue in Tuba? Do you not think your nearest kin would seek to avenge your death? And think also on this – what if you are next? Two brothers slain in order. Can't you see a pattern in all this?'

'Sister, sister, do not go on so. You are reading more into this than it warrants. Yes, my brothers are dead and both died by violent means. But that is mere coincidence. We all have to die. This is a violent time we live in. Why, only last week an outlaw gang held up a train at Blaxton and killed the guardsman.'

In his agitation Big John rose and paced up and down the room. He was about to continue when Dorothy spoke out.

'John, our nephew, Richard, grows fat on the acquisition of the Grant holdings. Because Tom and I have no children of our own Richard was named in Tom's will as his executor. With Tom's share of the business he now becomes the chief shareholder. Can't you see a pattern in all this? We have to act now and bring all this out in the open.'

John Grant sat down heavily in his leather-bound chair. There was a weary look about the old man.

'What you say may all be true. But what proof have we that Richard was involved in the deaths of our brothers. I cannot move against him without concrete evidence.'

'Whom do I complain to then?' interrupted his interlocutor.

'To God, the widow's champion and defence,' her brother-in-law answered.

'Why then, I will. John Grant, you are lucky in having a strong son. Perhaps Harry will act as a bulwark and save you from the worst excesses of Richard. Is he not here?'

'No, he is out riding somewhere. We had a bunch of steers go missin'. He's trying to track 'em down. There's been a lot of rustlin' recently. It really annoys Harry. He hates to see the fruits of our toil drained off by thieves. I only hope he don't get himself in too much trouble.'

Harry's aunt smiled wryly.

'Your Harry can take care of himself. He is the son I would have wanted for myself. You tell him I called and tell him I was askin' for him.'

3

At that moment Harry Grant's thoughts were far from his aunt and, indeed, from his father Big John.

Harry Grant was a big man with broad muscular shoulders built up over years of hard physical work on the family cattle ranch. He had clear blue eyes and a square-jawed face. Right now those usually placid and amiable eyes were narrowed as he sat his horse above the river.

He was gazing down at the men working the cattle towards the ford. Once over the river he knew they would have a clear run down to the Mexican border.

The men were relaxed as they herded the cattle. They looked like any ordinary bunch of cowpokes going about their usual job of cow-herding. When a recalcitrant steer lagged behind or strayed away from the main bunch the cowboys chivvied it along and the riders were doing a reasonably good job of keeping the herd on the move.

Harry nudged his horse forward. The big

grey stallion lifted its head and started down the slope towards the river. It snorted gently as it smelt the water.

'All right, Prince, we could both do with a drink.'

Horse and rider had been travelling all night. The stallion was weary from lack of rest and sleep. Harry had not stopped for water or feed but had pushed on through the starlit hours. He also was weary but drove the thoughts of tiredness and food to the back of his mind.

The horse picked a path down towards the river. Harry's intention was to cut ahead of the herd and get to the river before the cattle arrived at the ford.

Dust hung in the morning air in the wake of the cattle herd. It made a hazy cloud that took a time to settle. Cattle and riders were coated in a fine powder. Some of the herders had pulled their bandannas up to cover nose and mouth.

Harry counted five riders with the herd. He estimated there were about 200 head of prime steers. By some standards the ratio of herders to cattle was a mite high. He figured experienced cowhands would have needed only a couple of them to handle a herd that size.

Arriving on the flat Harry urged his weary mount to greater efforts. He wanted to be at that ford when the herd arrived at the crossing.

The river Elkhorn was wide and slow. Countless wagons, riders and beasts had trodden a well-worn trail down to the river's edge. The trail could clearly be seen emerging on the other side. It was an ancient passageway beaten into a permanent track by herds of buffalo and deer over the centuries. Man had followed the herds on their migratory path and hunted these wild beasts to extinction. Now the cowboys drove their own beasts across those same paths that countless hoofs had cleared before them.

Harry reined in at the water's edge and swung down from his mount. He felt stiff and sore from too many hours in the saddle. The grey lowered its head to drink. Harry took out his water-bottle and emptied the contents into the river. He knelt by the water and refreshed his canteen. While he drank he squinted back up the trail towards the herd.

'Ten minutes at the most, Prince,' he informed the horse. The grey finished drinking and shifted its attention to a patch of grass growing by the river. Harry corked his canteen and took out the makings from his shirt pocket. He began to build a smoke. Then he gave his full attention to the oncoming herd and riders.

Anyone could have mistaken Harry Grant for an ordinary cowpoke. He wore a buckskin waistcoat over a plaid shirt. His faded Levis had seen better days. On his feet was a good pair of leather riding-boots. A gun belt slanted across his waist was weighed down on the right side by a pearl-handled Colt revolver in a leather holster. But Harry Grant was no ordinary ranch hand.

His father was Big John Grant, owner of one of the largest ranches in the county and Harry was his son and heir.

Big John was the patriarch of a large family. His brothers had branched out into various ventures and were all successful businessmen. The Grant family had become one of the most powerful and influential in the county.

While he smoked, almost without thinking about it, Harry Grant reached down and unhooked the rawhide thong holding his sidearm secure. He eased the Colt revolver in the holster to make sure it did not snag. There was a rifle in the saddle scabbard but he did not think he would need that.

The herd was closing steadily on the river. If anything they were moving somewhat faster now as the beasts sensed the water ahead.

Harry's smoke was well down as the first of the steers reached the water. They hesitated at the edge but the pressure of the herd pushed them on into the water. Bellowing and snorting the steers plunged in, kicking up spurts of water and creating small waves. The water churned as more and more of the herd entered the water.

Harry could see the riders bunching together as they rode up. They were staring in his direction. He made no acknowledgement of the men. His eyes were scrutinizing the steers as they pressed past him.

While the animals milled around in the river the herders walked their horses behind them, keeping any stragglers from roaming too far from the main herd. He could almost see the riders relaxing as they realized he was on his own. As far as they could make out he was just a drifter casually watching a herd of steers making a river crossing.

Harry weighed up the riders as they approached. The noise of water being churned up along with bellowing cattle was making quite a racket. He had to raise his voice to make himself heard.

'Howdy, fellas, tidy bunch of steers you got there. Where you headin'?'

4

A heavyset man with a full beard, turned his horse towards the lone cowboy. Harry had noted the big Colt .45 in the man's holster. All the men carried sidearms, which was not unusual in a country where rustlers and bandits sometimes operated. As well as the sidearms he had seen the carbines slung about the riders' saddles.

'Across the river.' The bearded man answered Harry's query.

'Yeah, I figured that out already. I mean after that. You fellas goin' down towards Mexico? I'm headin' that way m'self. Could use a little company. Fed up ridin' on my own.'

Harry waited. The bearded man took his time replying. By this time his horse had reached the river and was bowing its head to drink. The other riders angled over and eased their mounts into the shallows beside the bearded man. One of these was a lean-looking man with a huge moustache clustered on his upper lip. Harry's Aunt Dorothy, when she saw a moustache like this, referred to the growth as being like a rat hanging on a man's lip. The other was a slim, handsome youth with a meagre growth of down struggling to show on his lip.

'Just keep on ridin', cowpoke,' the big man said at last. 'We don't take to company.'

Harry nodded thoughtfully.

'You fellas ride for the Big G?'

The bearded man tensed and slid his right hand from the reins to rest on his thigh inches from the handle of the big Colt. His companions moved their horses sideways to form a half-circle facing towards the man standing on the bank. Harry could not see the other two riders. He guessed they were on the far side of the herd, keeping them from spreading out along the river.

The three riders stared hard at Harry. He stood there looking relaxed. Smoke from his cigarette drifted up across his face before dispersing into the air.

'You ask a lot of questions, fella.' The words were spoken as an accusation. 'Don't like nosy cowhands. You ever heard the sayin' – curiosity killed the cat?'

The horses shifted uneasily beneath their riders as if sensing the tension building up between the men. Harry Grant reached up slowly and took the cigarette stub from his mouth. He flicked the spent butt out into the river.

'Just bein' friendly. I used to ride for the Big G. Know that brand anywhere.'

'Dude, if you look closer you see the brand is Circle L. Now if your nosiness is finished just climb on your pony and ride on out of here. I suggest go back the way you came.' The bearded man pointed back up the trail down which they had just driven. The man on the ground nodded thoughtfully.

'I guess I will look a mite closer at them beeves.' As he spoke Harry made as if to move past the mounted men. The bearded man's hand now slid on to his gun butt. There was no mistaking the menace as his companions did likewise.

'Mister, just git on your horse and go while you're still able to.'

Harry stopped moving forward. Slowly he raised his hand and with one finger tipped the Stetson to the back of his head. A long strand of blond hair worked loose from under the brim of the hat.

'What's your beef, fella?' he asked. 'You got something to hide.'

'Son of a bitch, who the hell do you think you're talkin' to. Get on that blasted pony and hightail it out of here. Nobody questions Bill Tunsall.' The bearded man gripped the handle of his pistol but did not draw his weapon.

'You figurin' to shoot me?' Harry asked evenly. 'Five of you against one lone cowhand. Seems a mite unfair.'

'Aw, shoot him Bill and be done with it,' intervened the man with the ratlike moustache. 'We cain't afford to hang about here jawin' with some half-wit drifter. If'n you don't then I will.' The speaker laid his hand on his six-shooter.

'I wouldn't do that mister,' Harry said coldly, peering up at the men but still looking relaxed. With that the man's patience snapped. He cursed and pulled his gun.

Harry Grant's clear blue eyes went an icy hue. With a rapid movement he stepped sideways. Almost as the action was completed the Colt appeared in his right hand. The explosion of the shots startled the cattle milling about in the water. They began a panicked surge across the river. Some of the beasts were plunging and rearing and their frantic bellowing increased in volume.

The man who had drawn his gun on the lone cowboy was punched backwards in the saddle as the .45 fired. His horse skittered in panic as the man's weight shifted on the saddle. The horses in the group reared in alarm. Bill Tunsall got off one shot from his Colt as his horse plunged sideways. The man on the ground coolly shot him out of the saddle before he could regain control. The young surviving rider threw up his hands.

'Don' shoot, for gawd's sake!' he shouted. Harry Grant could not hear the words but he understood the man's actions.

'Throw your weapon down,' he shouted, waving the Colt at the rider. The man sensed Harry's meaning and disarmed – drawing and throwing down his pistol. Unlike his companions he did not carry a carbine. Harry stepped forward and kicked the revolver into the river. By now most of the cattle were across the other side of the river and beginning to quieten. The water had slowed them somewhat and there was no more shooting to spook them again.

Harry grabbed the reins of his mount. The well-trained stallion had remained standing patiently throughout the racket. Still keeping hold of the Colt he swung on to the saddle. From this vantage point he could now see the two remaining riders spurring up the river bank towards him. He waited patiently for their arrival. It didn't take them long to get there. They pulled up looking suspiciously at the man on the grey stallion.

'What the hell's goin' on, Luke?' The question was addressed to the young rider. Their eyes narrowed as they noticed the pistol in Harry Grant's hand. Then they saw the bodies sprawled by the river.

'Jeez!' Their eyes flicked between Luke and Grant. 'He gun Bill an' Tatum?'

The young rider nodded vigorously, never taking his eyes off Harry. As they eyed the lone cowboy the two newcomers let their hands stray towards their weapons. Both wore holstered pistols and the stocks of carbines poked up from saddle scabbards.

'What's goin' on?'

'These fellas drew on me.' Harry gestured with his Colt at the bodies. 'You fellas wanta take up where they left off?'

The question hung in the air between them. The two cow-herders nervously licked their lips. Their eyes flicked between their dead companions and the stranger.

'You shot 'em down in cold blood,' one of them ventured at last. 'Bill was fast with a gun. More'n likely you murdered him an' Tatum.'

Harry didn't bother to answer. He waited

29

patiently. The surviving cowboy of the original trio spoke at last.

'Weren't like that. Bill an' Tatum were figurin' on shootin' this fella. They drew first. This fella just gunned them down. It were all fair and square.'

An uneasy silence descended. Most of the cattle had settled down on the far side of the river. There was grass growing on that bank. They began to gaze contentedly.

'What the hell you want, fella? Ain't right to sneak up on folks going about their peaceable affairs and shoot them down.'

'That's right, fella. I was waterin' my horse, mindin' my own business when these cattle-rustlers decided to shoot me.'

All three stiffened.

'Cattle-rustlers – who you callin' rustlers?'

'My guess those cows came off the Big G. Someone made a poor job of rebrandin' – trying to change the Big G to circle L...'

The cowboys glanced uneasily at each other.

'We bought those steers legit. Don't know nothin' about any Big G. Paid good money too. Now if you put that gun up we can go on across the river and mosey on along down to our outfit. We need those steers to restock. Lost some steers to Injuns.' The man told the lie with a belligerent glint in his eye. He wheeled his horse around. 'Come on fellas. Time to take those cows home.'

'Hold it right there, cowboy. If'n' what you say is true then you don't mind showin' me that bill of sale for them critters.'

The man seemed to be having trouble controlling his horse. Harry couldn't see his hands as he wrestled with the reins. Then he was coming round fast. Even before he was fully turned his gun was spurting bullets at Harry. His companion whooped and pulled his gun also. The man they were shooting at was not where he should have been.

Harry Grant was off his horse and kneeling down behind the big stallion. Flame spurted from the barrel of his pistol. The first gunman took a couple of bullets in his chest. The whoop from his companion was cut short as a bullet bored into his throat. Both men flopped over in the saddle and were thrown to the ground as their mounts started bucking in fright.

Harry Grant stood. As he kept a wary eye on the stricken cowboys he was punching empty shells from his six-shooter. Swiftly he reloaded and then walked slowly forward. The only man to survive the gunfight was staring at his companions in horror.

'Jeez, man, you killed them all.' He was ashen-faced and his body was shaking. Suddenly he slid from his horse and, bending over, threw up into the grass. Harry Grant ignored the retching cowboy and walked to the bodies. For a few moments he studied the dead men.

'Guess your rustlin' days are over,' he said to no one in particular. Then he turned his attention to the surviving rustler.

'You finished pukin' up your breakfast?'

The cowhand straightened up and turned a grey face towards the speaker. He wiped a trembling hand across his mouth.

'You ... you figger on shootin' me too, mister?'

'I might,' drawled Harry, 'depends on your behaviour. I heard your friends call you Luke. What's your other moniker?'

'Luke Parsons.'

'Well, Luke, I'm Harry Grant. My pa, Big John Grant, owns the Big G. I bin trailin' you rustlers for the past few days. Now help me catch these mounts.'

Together they soon rounded up the rustlers' horses. They took a few more moments to remove saddles and bridles, then turned the animals loose. Harry and his unwilling helper laid the dead rustlers in a row some way back from the river.

'We cain't take them bodies with us. We'll collect their valuables and drop them into the sheriff in Lourdes. That's the nearest town to the Big G. You'll have to give him their names and any information to track their relatives.'

He eyed the young man. On close inspection he realized the rustler was no more than a boy. Harry guessed he wasn't yet twenty years old.

'You can help me git these steers back across the river,' Harry instructed him. They splashed across and easily retrieved the herd. The cattle were docile now they had been watered and had eaten a little grass.

'I aim to drive these steers back to the Big G, from where they came originally. You can make this easy or hard on yourself. Help me git them there an' I might put in a good word for you with the law.'

Harry Grant stared unwaveringly at the youngster. The young man shifted uncomfortably in his saddle and did not meet those hard, azure eyes.

'Yessir, I'll be real good.'

5

Richard Grant sat at a large, polished mahogany desk staring thoughtfully at the man sitting across from him. Like his cousin, Harry, Richard was a big, well-built man. That was as far as the similarity went. Where Harry was blond and had the bronzed glow of a man who spent most of his working day outdoors, his cousin was dark-haired but with a sallow complexion. He wore a well-tailored suit of dark broadcloth. His large manicured hands played thoughtfully with an ornate letter-opener.

'So Uncle Tom is dead. Slain by persons unknown.' Richard sighed. 'I suppose I'll have to offer my condolences to Aunt Dorothy. Not a task I look forward to. She always had an acid tongue. She never liked me. Not that I ever gave her cause to dislike me.' He smiled suddenly across at the man opposite. 'That is, till now, cousin.'

The man he addressed as cousin grinned back at Richard Grant. David Austin was a young man with thinning mousy hair and sported an untidy moustache and sparse beard. His mother and Richard's were sisters.

'It'll be a lovely funeral. I got a black suit I ain't wore since your weddin' day,' replied Austin. 'You know she's spreadin' all sorts of hoss-shit 'bout you. Is askin' why it is your uncles are all being killed and you're the beneficiary from their deaths.'

Richard Grant sighed again. He leaned forward and lifted the lid on a silver humidifier which was standing on his desk. After selecting a cigar from the container he nodded an invitation for his cousin to help himself.

'Aunt Dorothy is a dotin' old woman. No one in their right mind would take any notice of her ravin'. 'Sides, she's half-mad with grief. She probably won't last long anyway, now that Tom's dead. She's the least of our worries. There's bigger fish to fry.' He had taken a heavy lighter from the desktop and was busy applying it to the tip of his cigar. When he had it going to his satisfaction he slid the lighter across to his cousin. When Austin's cigar was exuding satisfying plumes of blue smoke he addressed his cousin.

'You amaze me, Richard. Your ambition seems boundless. You own virtually all of Lourdes includin' the bank and all the big

35

businesses that count. You stand to take over Tom Grant's spread now that he's out of the way. You are the mayor of the town with the town committee in your pocket, not to mention Sheriff Garrison and Judge Burton. What more is there to aim for?'

Richard Grant smiled across the desk at Austin.

'One thing stops me from ownin' the whole county and that's the Big G.'

David Austin was just inhaling the aromatic smoke from his cigar. He choked and then went into a spasm of coughing. When at last he surfaced he wiped tears from his eyes.

'Jeez, Richard, don't make cracks like that while I'm smokin'. You know as well as I do Uncle John will never sell the Big G. He spent his whole life out on that ranch buildin' it up from scratch. You stand as much chance of getting hold of the Big G as I have of runnin' for president.'

'You didn't say anythin' like that when I told you what I wanted done to get my hands on Uncle Tom's spread.'

David Austin stared back across at his cousin with widening eyes. When he spoke it was in a low tremulous voice.

'No, Richard. Tell me I'm imaginin'

things. I didn't hear you correct.'

Richard Grant leaned towards his cousin to emphasize his next words.

'Do I need to spell it out for you? I want the Big G. With that acquisition I'll own virtually the whole county. I'll be the most powerful man in the territory. Next stop governor!' He leaned back in his chair and sucked at his cigar. Through clouds of smoke he continued: 'And after governor...' he threw apart his hands in an all-embracing gesture. '...the state – the senate...?' He trailed off and stared at the other man.

'But Uncle John...!' David Austin shook his head in disbelief. 'You're not talkin' sense, Richard. This is a step too far.'

Richard Grant leaned back in his chair and placed both hands behind his head. He blew cigar smoke at the ceiling.

'You ever heard of William Shakespeare?'

David Austin nodded. 'He were some old English queen used to write poetry.'

'That's right, David. We had an old cowhand on our place and he used to read me bits of this Shakespeare. There was this Scottish fella. His name were Lord Macbeth. Well, he had a similar problem to me. People were in his way. So he...' Richard Grant made the shape of a gun with his thumb and forefinger, 'bamb, bamb, killed them himself or hired someone to do it for him. There was one line in that play that always stayed with me. Even now all these years later I remember it.' The speaker swivelled his chair to and fro as he intoned the quotation from the play. '"I have waded so deep in blood it would be harder to turn back than carry on." Well, them's the words near enough.'

Richard Grant gazed into the far distance as he fell silent. It was as if he was going back to those years as a boy or perhaps looking forward to his coming reign as the most powerful man in the county. At last he stopped his chair and looked quizzically at his companion.

'That's me, David. I'm in too deep now to go back. The Big G will become my property whatever it takes.'

'For all you say, Richard, its not going to do you any good. You still have Cousin Harry to deal with.'

Richard Grant began to swivel his chair again. Thoughtfully he sucked on his cigar. He blew a cloud of smoke into the air.

'Cousin Harry – tough old Cousin Harry.'

'You're damn right he's tough. If you're thinkin' of takin' on Harry Grant I wish you luck. He's not some old man like Uncle Tom and Uncle Glenn. He's tough as a wolverine. In fact it wouldn't surprise me if his ma lay with a wolf before he was whelped.'

Richard Grant smiled at his cousin.

'David, David, David. It never fails to surprise me what a coward you are. There are more ways to skin a cat than flies on a cow-chip. Harry is the main target. With him out of the way old John will be an easy ride.'

'Jeeze, Richard, I might be a coward but there are times you scare the pants off'n me.'

Richard Grant laughed out loud then.

'Good. Good. Just you be my eyes and ears and errand-boy, David, and you have no need ever to fear me.'

And David Austin, rather than being reassured by these words, felt a deep chill in his bones. He did not meet Richard Grant's eyes as he replied.

'You know I'm your man soul and body.' He forced himself to look up at his cousin. 'But Harry Grant is a different type of cat all together. He's more like a cougar than a tabby. I wouldn't want to tangle with him. You know he's pals with that marshal over in Toska. Rumour has it he asked Harry to help him out against a nest of outlaws that had been plaguin' the area with robberies and killin's. Made him deputy and they rode out against the bunch – just the two o' them. They brought back just two for hangin'. The rest is dead or still runnin'.'

Richard Grant smiled at the speaker.

'The tougher they are the more satisfyin' the crash when they go down. Let me tell you somethin', Cousin, there's no one can stand in my way. I'm on my way to the top. Do you think I'll allow some cowhand who thinks he's a ring-tailed bobcat stand in my way? No, no, Cousin David, I'll be king here and any what cares to challenge me will get ploughed under.'

Richard Grant stared at his companion as if challenging him to contradict him. But David Austin kept quiet. He would never openly challenge anyone. A knife in a dark alley or a shot from a safe distance was more his way. Also he was fully confident that his cousin would accomplish all he set out to do with or without him. He wanted to be with the king at the feast. In keeping with his nature he would allow others to do the risky work and then slink in like a coyote to tear at the dead body.

'You ever heard of Jonah Jones?' Richard

Grant suddenly asked him.

David's eyebrows rose as he contemplated his cousin.

'Who the hell hasn't heard of Jonah Jones? He's a killer spawned straight out of hell. It's said he'll kill anyone or anythin' for a price. What the hell sort of question's that?'

'What would you do if you knew he was comin' for you?'

'Do! I'd hightail it to Mexico and git a boat for South America. Then I'd git on a boat for Europe. I'd change my name and git the transcontinental express to the remotest boundary of Russia. By that time if I had any funds left I'd hire a squadron of Cossacks to patrol my house twenty-four hours a day an' even then I still wouldn't feel safe.'

Richard Grant laughed out loud.

'I figger you have the right of it. Anyway, that's the man I want you to contact.'

6

Dusk was drawing a light veil over the sky as a prelude to the sun's going down. Harry Grant had been looking for a likely place to bed the cattle down for the night.

He knew they weren't far from the main trail which ran through to Toska. Passenger coaches passed that way. Though with the coming of the railway they were slowly going out of business. Some still clung to the out-of-the-way routes. He had no idea of the timetable for the coaches. He was hoping that if one came along he could hand his rustler companion over for transportation to his friend, Marshal Ben North, in Toska.

The herd ambled along without much bother. Harry did not drive them on. He knew they had been pushed hard enough in the last week, for the rustlers would have been in a hurry to vacate the area of their crime.

Up ahead he saw a shallow depression at the bottom of a small hill. The hollow was well grassed. If he made camp on the hill he could keep an eye out for any trouble with the steers. He did not anticipate any bother. His main problem was his delinquent rustler. The sooner he got shot of him the easier he would sleep.

He rode ahead to the brow of the hill and was gratified to see the outline of the Toska trail. The camp would serve two purposes. He could survey the herd from there and also spot a coach if one passed by, which would give him the prospect of ridding himself of his unwanted helper. Satisfied with his choice he rode down to the young rustler to tell him of his decision to make camp.

Up till then the youngster had given no bother. He had fallen in without argument with Harry's plans. The boy was subdued and thoughtful. Harry assumed he was contemplating his not too rosy future. If he was tried for rustling there was a possibility he might be hanged. This was cattle country. The law tended to be harsh in such matters. In some counties a rustler might get away with a jail sentence, but here it was viewed much more seriously.

'Reckon we'll bed down here for the night,' he called out. 'No point in riskin' a night drive. We ain't in any hurry. You settle them down.' He pointed up the hill. 'I'll git a fire goin' – git the coffee on.'

The youngster waved acknowledgement and Harry cantered back up the hill to pick a campsite. He found a reasonably flat area screened on one side by some bushes. Before seeking his own comforts he off-saddled and allowed Prince his freedom. He rarely tethered the big stallion. As far as Harry was concerned the horse was his sentry. In the past the stallion had warned him of impending danger.

As he was rubbing down the big horse he saw the dust sign. A smile of satisfaction lit his face for an instant. A vehicle was approaching along the Toska road.

'Look at that, Prince. With a bit of luck, that's a stagecoach headin' for Toska. Maybe they can be persuaded to take young Luke Parsons off'en our hands.'

He watched the dust for a few moments to estimate its speed. It was coming along at a leisurely pace. Harry looked regretfully at the discarded saddle. Deciding it was too much trouble to saddle up again he retrieved his rifle. Then he vaulted on to Prince's back. He had no intention of leaving the gun for the young rustler to find when he arrived at the campsite.

The stallion looked round balefully at him as if to say: I thought we were finished for the day. Harry searched for his outlaw helper. The rustler was riding around the herd, keeping them nicely bunched up. He smiled ruefully If he got rid of his cowhand it would be a more difficult drive back to the Big G. He turned the stallion and rode down to intercept the coach.

The hill leading down to the roadway was studded with trees. Harry made slow progress as he wove his way down the slope. As a result he did not realize that the oncoming vehicle had stopped moving until he was on the main trail.

'Damn, I hope the thing ain't broke down,' he muttered and set the stallion towards the stalled coach. As he grew closer he was able to make out more details. He could see a couple of horsemen dismounted, then, squinting ahead, he realized that the vehicle was not a coach but a buggy of some kind.

'Damn,' he muttered again. A private individual would not be inclined to take a rustler on board. Nevertheless he pushed on. He could just make out that there were three or four people and they were milling about at the side of the buggy.

Frowning, he squinted in order to see better. The gathering dusk did not make it easy to make out details. If he wasn't mistaken some sort of struggle was taking place. He kicked his heels into the stallion's sides and as he did so a scream carried faintly across the evening air.

'Goddamn it, Prince what the hell's happenin'?' He was sure it was a woman who screamed. Even as he swore he set the stallion in a dead run towards the group. At the same time he discharged his rifle. He wasn't aiming at anything – it was just a warning shot. And by distracting the group he just might prevent someone getting injured.

The stallion bounded along the trail, raising its own little dust train in its wake. By now the group were looking towards the sound of the shot. Harry could make out three men. Someone was lying on the ground. He groaned inwardly. His arrival was too late to help the poor woman. Then the men were shooting at him.

Harry didn't slacken speed. Instead he raised the rifle and began firing at the little group. He knew he had little chance of hitting anyone but with any luck it would spoil the shooters' aim. When Harry was close enough for a gun duel he pulled up in a cloud of trail dust.

The men at the buggy saw Harry emerge from the dust with the rifle held at waist-level. Harry started firing again. One man spun around and slumped against the side of the buggy. His companions looked at him, then ran round to the back of the carriage to their horses and fumbled to untie reins. The wounded man stumbled after them.

Harry kept on firing but was deliberately firing wide. He didn't want to kill anyone until he knew what was going on. The killings at the river crossing were enough to last him a lifetime. At the river he had shot in self-defence. Now he only wanted to drive the men away.

At last the men sorted out the horses. Harry watched as they urged their mounts into a gallop back the way they had come. One horse was riding double. The wounded man had clambered on behind one of the riders.

Harry ran the last few yards to the woman. She was sitting up by now. Harry stopped and gawked. He could not help himself. It was not every day a man came upon a semi-nude woman out on the range.

Her clothing had been torn from her upper body revealing the soft swell of full breasts. Her dress was rucked up above her waist and he was given a full view of plump thighs. The woman was vainly struggling to cover herself with her ripped blouse and at the same time jerking her dress down to cover her legs. To his shame Harry Grant just stood and ogled. It was the sound of the woman's sobbing that brought back his manners.

Averting his eyes he moved to the buggy. He put down his gun and grabbed a rug from the rig. He shuffled backwards to the sobbing woman and without looking around held out the rug.

'Here ma'am, this here blanket might help.'

The sobbing lessened, then he felt the rug lifted from his hand. For the life of him he could not think what to do next. Harry Grant was no ladies' man at the best of times. Usually he found himself tongue-tied and left footed in female company. Now he was alone on the Toska road with a half-naked woman and he was completely lost.

'Please Gawd,' he said inwardly, 'I'm not a prayin' man but just get me outta this an' I'll go to church next Sunday.' Then, thinking that that wasn't sufficient to tempt God's intervention he added: 'I'll put ten dollars in the collection box.'

'Halloa there, Mr Grant. Everything all right up here.'

Considering that he was figuring ways and means of getting rid of his helper, Harry at that moment would have embraced the young rustler now for this intervention. Gratefully he turned towards the young outlaw. The rustler was gawking just as Harry had minutes before.

'Damn you, Luke,' he said through gritted teeth. He was careful not to turn around to look at the object of Luke's staring.

'Luke, is it you?' a quavering female voice asked.

'Allison ... what the hell ... where did you come from?'

'Oh, Luke...!

A blanket-clad figure stumbled past Harry. Luke almost fell from his mount as he jumped down. Then they were in each other's arms.

'Luke, Luke.' The woman was sobbing and saying the name over and over.

Harry Grant stood totally perplexed at this unexpected turn of events. He opened his mouth to speak but could think of nothing to say so he closed it again. As before it was the rustler who saved the situation for him. Still holding the sobbing woman he looked over her head at Harry.

'What happened, Mr Grant? I heard the shootin' and came to see.'

Before Harry could answer the woman disentangled herself from Luke's embrace. She turned to Harry. He found himself staring into the greenest of eyes. They were soft and tear-filled and they sent a thrill down his spine.

'Mr Grant, is that your name?'

Clutching the blanket tightly around her she stared up at him. Dumbly he nodded. He was expecting a coarse woman of the saloon breed. The woman before him was coated with dust and grime from rolling around in the dirt of the road. Her hair – the reddest hair he had ever seen – was in a wild tangle. She was clad in a dirty old horse-blanket. But to Harry Grant she was the most beautiful creature he had ever beheld.

For the time being he was struck dumb. He wished he were somewhere else and yet at the same time he was glad to be here.

The vision turned and took Luke's arm. She held on to it as she spoke. Harry Grant felt a stab of jealousy as he saw the girl holding on to the boy's arm.

'Mr Grant saved me. Those men were ... they tried to...' she took a deep shuddering breath before continuing: 'they were about to ... to ... they were attacking me when Mr Grant showed up...'

'What the hell! Jeez ... Allison ... oh God!'

Then they were both staring at Harry Grant and his awkwardness increased.

'I ... aw ... mebby we should git back to our camp. I ... aw ... will you drive the lady back, Luke, while I take the horses?'

Harry Grant was walking round on wooden legs making noises with a wooden tongue. He gestured towards the buggy. Somehow he found himself on top of Prince with the reins of Luke's mount in his hand. The horses headed back to the hill where he had intended to set up camp.

He had started off disliking the young rustler, hoping to get rid of him on a coach. Now, every time he remembered that embrace he was beginning to hate him. Powerful emotions swirled around inside his head as he listened to the sound of the buggy following. The rumble of voices from the two young people behind was like a saw-blade rasping on his heart.

7

Harry Grant sat beside the fire nursing a mug of coffee. Opposite him sat the young couple, deeply engrossed in talk. He was angry with himself.

In spite of all his admonitions to himself he felt a stab of jealousy each time he inadvertently looked across the camp-fire. He tortured himself by eyeing the way the girl's hand rested so intimately on the rustler's arm as they talked. Their voices were low and subdued. Harry could not hear the conservation.

'I'll see him hanged,' he muttered. But there was no conviction in the sentiment. Abruptly he stood. 'I'll take first watch,' he called out to the couple. He slung the dregs of coffee, walked across and began to saddle Prince.

'I'll wake you in the night to do the last few hours till dawn,' he called over his shoulder. He walked Prince away from the camp.

Harry Grant did not expect any bother

from the herd. Tired from their forced drive to the river crossing, they now had an opportunity to rest and graze. He was reassured by the general quietness pervading the herd. The depression he had chosen was ideal for keeping the herd together. They had settled down for the night and he believed none of the beasts would want to wander in the dark.

Slowly he circled the herd, totally oblivious of his surroundings. For the first time in his young life Harry Grant paid scant attention to the task he had been doing all his life on his father's ranch. He rode his horse to a rise in the ground and stared out at the night sky. His mind was a turmoil of emotions.

'Gawdamn, what's the matter with me?'

Beneath him Prince bent his head and snuffled round for something to eat.

Harry knew what was the matter. He could not rid his mind of images of soft, pale flesh. No matter what he did a pair of naked, thrashing legs and the soft swell of female breasts intruded on his imagination.

'Allison.' He said the name out loud into the night, then looked round guiltily as if he would be overheard; then realizing he was alone he said it again. 'Allison.'

Immediately he saw again the way she had

run to Luke and flung her arms around him.

'Wait till the law catches up with him and then she mightn't be so keen on him.'

As he muttered this a wave of guilt swept over him and he knew he couldn't bring himself to condemn the young rustler. It was why he didn't tell the girl about Luke's shady past. Even though the pangs of jealousy bit deep he wouldn't be the one to disillusion her.

He sighed deeply as he sank deeper and deeper into depression. When the time came he would just say farewell and watch Allison and her beau ride out of his life.

'Maybe she'll think on me sometime. After all I did save her from those bastard no-goods.' A hot wave of anger swept through him as he remembered the three men. 'If'n I ever come across them low-life they'll regret it.'

He couldn't bring himself to go back to the camp.

He dismounted and unsaddled Prince. Then he tossed the horse-blanket to the ground and lay on his back, staring up at the stars. His mind swirled round and round and the hollow feeling in the pit of his stomach was not from lack of food.

'Dammit,' he groaned. He did not feel like sleep. A long night stretched ahead of him.

A pair of moist green eyes gazed into his. He reached out and ran his hand through a luxuriant mass of red hair. Wet velvety lips pushed against his face. 'Allison,' he whispered, 'is it really you?' She snuffled into his ear. He moaned and opened his eyes.

'Prince, for Gawd's sake what the hell'er you doin?'

Harry sat up abruptly, furiously wiping horse slobber from his face. Prince regarded him gravely. If he believed horses capable of humour Harry could have swore there was a twinkle in Prince's eye.

He stared around him in some bewilderment. Dawn was edging the horizon with gold ribbons. If he had been in a more receptive mood Harry would have spent a moment or two admiring this splendour of nature.

'Dammit,' he sighed. 'I must have fallen asleep.'

He had lain awake most of the night, eventually falling into an uneasy doze only to be rudely awakened by Prince's amorous attentions.

Though he was reluctant to go back to the camp and face the two lovers, nevertheless the welfare of the herd was paramount. The sooner the rescued cattle were back on Big G range the better. Also, the longer he was away, the more worried his father would be.

The herd was still contentedly gathered together as he rode towards the campsite. He was puzzled somewhat as to why his helper had not come looking for him. After all, he had told the rustler he would expect him to do his share of night herding. As he neared the vicinity of the campsite the distinct lack of smoke from a fire concerned him.

'Lazy good-fer-nothin' rustler.'

A pang of jealous anger struck deep as he thought what might keep the rustler abed so late in the morning. And then he cursed and urged Prince into a gallop. At the campsite he hauled up.

'Gawdamn, stinkin', sneakin' rustler.'

Harry stared at the deserted camp and the anger built up in him. The rustler and the red-haired girl were gone. So too were the buggy and the girl's belongings.

8

It was late afternoon as Harry Grant rode into the yard of the Big G. As he expected, Big John stood on the veranda watching his son ride in. Harry pulled up and slid off Prince.

'Howdy, son. You're a welcome sight. Everythin' all right?'

Harry grunted and turned to lead Prince to the corral. His father spun around and walked back into the house. He would expect a full report from Harry. Shortly after his homecoming they were sitting in the living-room drinking coffee and smoking.

'An' that's it,' Harry finished up. 'I put the cattle down in the south pasture. Don' seem much the worse for their travels.'

He had told the old man everything except for the girl and the young rustler. On the lonely ride back he had come to terms with his anger and tangled emotions.

'Gawdamn, Harry, I don' like you goin' off like that on your own. What if'n one of those damned rustlers winged you? I know you can look after yourself. I raised you to be tough and independent. But sometimes you act a mite foolish. You could have come back and gotten some of the boys to ride with you.'

'Wasn't time, Pa. Hell, if'n I hadn't gotten to that river crossin' afore them they'da been well on the way to Mexico by now.'

His father grumbled and muttered something Harry couldn't make out. But he knew Big John was pleased with him.

The old man was extremely proud of his son. And Harry in turn loved his father with a deep and enduring affection. He couldn't remember his mother. His father had raised him and a deep bond existed between the two men.

'There's something else.' Harry hesitated a moment before continuing: 'I ... sorta ... came across this girl and her beau. They were being set on by some rough-necks. We managed to chase them off. They camped one night with me and then rode on in the mornin'.'

Harry was uncomfortable lying to his old man. He stared into his coffee so did not see the shrewd look Big John gave his son. Big John knew when to pry and when to ease back. He knew there was more to the tale than Harry was letting on but he wasn't going to press him on the matter.

'What were their names?'

'He said his name was Luke Parsons and the girl ... were Allison. Damned if I can remember what she said her second name were.'

The truth was Harry didn't know. He had been too flustered after that traumatic first meeting to ask and he couldn't recall the girl offering anything other than her first name. He grinned at his father.

'Could'a bin Allison Allison.' But Big John could detect a faint hint of perplexity behind Harry's smile.

A few hours later Harry and Big John were headed for town. Harry wanted to have some recreation after his hectic days on the trail of the rustlers. He was determined to get stinking drunk tonight and forget the green-eyed redhead who haunted his dreams.

The Hot Spur was owned by Richard Grant. It was a large, prosperous establishment. A well-stocked bar catered for most tastes in liquor while a grand stage provided song and dance routines. Roulette and card-games catered for the gamblers. Richard Grant had even had a billiard-table imported to give the establishment some class.

Saloon girls circulated freely amongst the customers, cadging drinks and selling the delights of their bodies. The saloon was only one of Richard Grant's enterprises. He owned the bank, the freight yard, the general store and indeed any business that was liable to make him money.

Big John and his son found a spot at the bar. As they were ordering Richard Grant intervened.

'No charge for these gentlemen,' he called out to the barman. He turned a smiling face to the two men. 'Uncle John and Cousin Harry, I ain't set eyes on you in a month of Sundays. You cattlemen must love those steers too much to leave 'em.'

'Howdy, Richard. I was gonna say we cain't afford the fancy prices in the Hot Spur to come in too often.'

Richard Grant laughed. He turned to the barman who was setting up two schooners of beer.

'Cigars for these gents.' He took one himself and stayed to bandy words, then left his relations to their evening's entertainment.

'I wonder what your Aunt Dorothy would say if'n she could see us confabbin' with her least-favourite nephew.'

'She still goin' on about Richard havin' a hand in the death of Uncle Tom?'

''Fraid so.' John Grant sighed. 'I don't think she'll ever get over it. By the way, she was askin' after you. Says at least she has one nephew she can be proud of.'

Neither of them took notice of the tall, cadaverous man dressed in shabby black clothes who walked up to the bar and stood a few paces from them.

Though he had come into town with the intention of getting drunk Harry restricted his drinks to beer. As he lounged against the bar and jawed with his father Harry's attention was only partly on the conversation.

The talk was general patter about ranch matters and Harry's success in returning the stolen herd. While he chatted part of his mind was seeing a beautiful young girl flinging herself into the arms of a rustler. He tried to blot out that other image of a pair of flailing legs and soft breasts. Try as he might and drink as he did, those images were to the forefront of his mind. Suddenly his thoughts were rudely interrupted when Big John was jostled from behind and spilled half his drink.

'What the hell?' the big man exclaimed, half-turning to see who had cannoned into him. 'Son of a bitch, you done spilled my drink.'

A tall man in a dark suit stared moodily from under the brow of a dusty black hat.

'Watch your mouth, cowboy. I ain't no son of a bitch, though you look as if a sow sired you.'

Big John blinked and stared at the stranger. His face flushed as the insult sunk home. Harry tensed. He could see trouble in this encounter. To him the man looked sinister and dangerous.

'Easy on, Big John, it's only a spilled drink. Let it go.'

But John Grant had, unlike his son, been sinking whiskey after whiskey and was three-quarters drunk.

'Let it go! Damned if I will. This son of a bitch spills my drink and then insults me. I ain't lettin' nothin' go.'

The 'son of a bitch' stepped back a few paces. His coat swung open to expose a Colt slung low on his gun belt.

'That's twice you called me. Take it back, or I'll stop that foul old mouth with a piece of lead.'

Around the trio there was sudden

scampering as the crowd, sensing trouble, backed off to a safe distance.

Big John blinked. He never would run away from trouble. Often he had boasted that he had fought everything that walked from Injuns to wolves to outlaws. He was drunk – he was old – but he still went for his gun.

Harry had no time to think. Even as he saw the stranger's gun appear as if by magic he reacted instinctively. There was a schooner of beer in his hand. He flung it at the gunman. As it flew through the air Harry noted that strangely enough the stranger's gun was pointed not at his father but at him. The man ducked as the beer-glass arced towards him and his shot went wild. Harry's gun was in his hand. He fired on reflex and saw the man stagger back. The gunman's hand came up again but abruptly his eyes glazed over and he sank into the sawdust on the floor.

Harry held his Colt trained on the still figure for a moment more. A groan and a thud behind swung him round to see Big John sitting on the floor, his back against the bar. His hands were clamped across his chest. Blood pumped from between his fingers. The old man's face was drained of colour. Harry shoved his gun away and quickly knelt beside his father.

'Jeez, Pa, you've been hit.' For a moment he stared helplessly at the blood, then he leapt into action. He grabbed a cloth from the bar and knelt again to press the pad against the blood.

'Get the sawbones,' he yelled out.

The sudden paralysis that had gripped the crowd was broken by his shout. The saloon began to buzz again as people crowded round to gawk at the downed men.

'OK Dad, someone's gone for Doc Fleming. Hang on in there.'

'Son of a bitch,' the big man groaned. 'This hurts like hell.'

Harry's heart squeezed within him. Big John had always been there – seemingly indestructible. Now he lay in a saloon wounded in a barroom brawl. It made no sense.

'Make way, git these people away from here.' The irascible voice of Doc Fleming sent a wave of relief through Harry.

'You old varmint, I thought you'd be too old for saloon fightin'.' Even as he spoke the doctor was kneeling beside the wounded man. Big John managed a weak smile.

'They tol' me you was retired, Doc. I just wanted to find out if'n you was.'

'You could have come an' asked, you old fool, without going to all this trouble.'

'Gawdamn, Harry, this is terrible.' Richard Grant appeared at Harry's side. 'An' to happen in my place. Jeez, Harry, I'm sorry. Is it bad?'

'Bad enough.'

'I've sent for Sheriff Garrison.'

Almost on cue the portly figure of the sheriff elbowed through the crowd.

'What's goin' on here?'

'This fella here shot Big John.' Harry indicated the man sprawled on the floor. 'I had to shoot him to stop him puttin' one in me too.'

He did not like the new sheriff. Richard Grant, who claimed he needed law and order to protect businesses in the town, had imported the man.

'More'n likely to administer his own version of law and order,' his aunt had declared. But no one listened to an embittered old woman.

'I'll have to arrest you, Mr Grant. Cain't have random killin' in Lourdes.'

'What ... I just tol' you he tried to kill us and you want to arrest me.'

'It's for a court to decide what happened. I'm just the law around here. Now if'n you just hand over that gun we'll mosey down to the jailhouse.'

For the first time Harry noticed the two deputies flanking the sheriff. They were mean-looking men with hard eyes. Both carried shotguns in a seemingly casual way. But Harry noticed that the muzzles were pointing in his direction. He tried once more to reason with the lawman.

'Gawdamn it, Sheriff, the man jumped us. Why the hell should I just let him gun down Big John an' m'self?'

'Just come quiet, son.' The sheriff was implacable. 'Don't want no trouble now, do we. There's been trouble enough with one man dead and one wounded. You'll have a fair trial.'

'Git some blankets to carry this man.' The doctor interrupted the exchange. 'Want him down at my place.' He turned to Harry. 'He'll be all right, Harry. Plenty of blood but touched no vitals.'

A hand lighted on Harry's shoulder and he swung round to see Richard Grant by his side.

'Harry, please, no more trouble. Go with Sheriff Garrison. You'll have the best lawyer money can buy. And I'll keep an eye on Uncle John. We'll do everythin' to git him better.'

For a moment the two men stared at each other. Then Harry sighed and his shoulders slumped. He fished his gun out of the holster and carefully handed it to the sheriff. As he did so he saw the sheriff relax and release the butt of his holstered revolver.

Men came forward with the blankets. With Doc Fleming cautioning them to be careful the wounded man was lifted onto the makeshift stretcher.

Harry reached out and touched his father on the cheek.

'You be good, Pa. Don't give Doc no bother.'

'I'll be all right, son. Just you watch your back.'

As Sheriff Garrison escorted Harry Grant from the saloon Richard Grant turned and looked on as the body of Jonas Jones was carried to the rear of the building to await transfer to the morgue. There was a faint smile on his handsome features. He cut a cigar and applied a sulphur head.

'Dead men tell no tales,' he muttered to no one in particular. Then he raised his voice. 'Sorry about the ruckus, gents. Drinks on the house. Let's git this place back to normal.'

9

Six years! Harry Grant sat in his cell, his mind in a whirl. Six years! The judge had at first inclined to ten years but then because of his father's pleading and his own previous good character it had been reduced to six. Harry was still shocked by the appearance of Big John at the trial.

Overnight his dad had become an old man. He looked pathetic and feeble as he pleaded with the judge not to take his son from him. In fairness the judge had reduced the original ten-year sentence. But for the twenty-year-old, it might as well have been twenty-six years. His six years' incarceration stretched into the future. A rattle of keys interrupted his morbid thoughts.

The deputy with the squint slouched into the cell area. He carried a shotgun which he kept pointed at the man in the cell. Behind him stood Sheriff Morrison, also holding a shotgun.

'Prison wagon's arrived. Time for you to go.'

Harry stood and waited for the cell door to be unlocked. He wore wrist- and leg-manacles. I'm just a hardened criminal as far as they're concerned, he thought. Squinty motioned him forward. Harry shuffled out into the corridor. The shotgun poked him in the back.

'Just keep walking. Any funny stuff and I'll save the state the cost of your board an' lodgin'.'

Harry blinked in the bright sunlight. A shove from behind sent him stumbling on to the boardwalk. Before him on the roadway stood an enclosed wagon. The driver sat in the front holding the reins of the horse team. Beside him a burly guard pointed his carbine down at the prisoner. At the rear of the vehicle another armed guard stood waiting by an open tailgate.

A buckboard drove across the road. Big John sat slumped in the seat. Harry raised his manacled hands in greeting. He swung round to face the sheriff.

'Can I say goodbye to my pa?'

The sheriff scowled. 'Yeah, I guess so. But be quick.'

Harry stepped out on to the roadway. He did not look round but he guessed every gun in front of the jail was pointed at him.

His spine tingled with the weight of all that lead aimed at him.

'Son, I'm real sorry about all this. I tried everythin' to save you...'

Harry held up his manacled hands to stem the flow of apologies.

'Pa, it's not your fault.' Before he could continue a voice was calling to him.

'Mr Grant, Mr Grant. Is that you?'

Harry turned and his heart did a sudden somersault. He stared in disbelief as the young woman hurried across to him. One hand was hanging on to her bonnet. Beneath the hat a mass of red tresses fluttered in the wind stirred by her passage. Allison, he said mentally, where in hell did you spring from? She was beside him now, staring up into his face. He was swimming in those misty green eyes.

'Mr Grant,' she pleaded, 'its Luke, they're takin' him to the penitentiary.'

Harry opened his mouth to speak but he never got to say anything. There was a yell from behind him.

'Allison, Allison.'

They both turned and looked towards the back of the prison wagon. A head was sticking out of the back door. Harry recognized the young rustler. The girl took a few faltering steps. Then she turned back to Harry. For the first time she noticed the manacles. Those lovely green eyes opened wider and her hand flew to her mouth. Harry was helpless as he watched the eyes swimming in tears. He gestured feebly with his bound hands. Then the tears in the green eyes overflowed.

'You too. They're sendin' you away also. What am I to do? You and Luke are the only people I know here. Now you are both being locked away.'

The guards were waving impatiently with their weapons.

'Time's up, kid. Time to go. Move it or we'll drag you behind the wagon.'

Harry turned desperately to his father.

'Pa, would you look after this young woman. She's the girl I told you about. The one I met on the trail.'

'I told you, boy, get over here now.'

'She ain't got nobody, Dad. Take care of her.'

A rifle hit him on the top of the head. Harry grunted with pain and almost went down. He turned and stumbled to the wagon.

'Don't worry about Luke,' he called over his shoulder.

The girl was standing in the middle of the

road. His heart was breaking to see her there, tears spilling down her cheeks. A gun barrel dug painfully into his back. He fell into the back of the wagon. The tailgate slammed shut and he heard the driver yell at the horses. He fell full length as the wagon lurched forward. A voice spoke up from the semi-darkness.

'Mr Grant, you all right, Mr Grant?'

10

Harry groaned. He groped around in the gloomy interior trying to get his bearings. A pair of hands reached out and helped him on to a wooden bench running the length of the prison wagon. He muttered thanks, guessing it was Luke Parsons.

His head was pounding from the blow it had received. But worse than that pain was the agonizing picture of Allison standing in the middle of the road as she watched her boyfriend being taken away. Frustration built within him as he realized that the rustler had brought this on himself, but worse, he had dragged his girlfriend along and now she was stranded. He could only hope that Big John would do as he had requested and look after the young girl.

Jeez, he thought, she's no more'n a kid.

'Mr Grant, what you doin' here?'

At last, through the turmoil of his emotions, he became aware of Luke Parsons speaking to him.

'Uh-huh.' He gathered his thoughts.

'More important, what the hell are you doin' in here?'

It was some moments before the reply came.

'You ... ah ... you remember that incident when I first met up with you? Well, I'd be obliged if you didn't say nothin' about that.'

Harry thought about this for a bit.

'OK. I take it your old habits had nothin' to do with your present situation.'

'Hell no. In fact if it were made knowed I might be in worse trouble.'

'So what the hella' you doin' here?'

'Those men you chased off – the ones that attacked Allison. Well, that were their buggy. She hired them to take her to Alaposa. The buggy-owner, he opined she needed protection on the trail so he hired the other two. Only they was cousins or brothers or somethin'. They planned to take all her belongin's, kidnap her and sell her on to a brothel or somethin'. Then you came along and spoilt all that. They came alookin' for us. Caught up with us in Alaposa. Spun the marshal a yarn as we'd hired the buggy an' then stole it. They let Allison off her being a woman an' all.'

'You have all the luck of a Pony Express rider with a case of haemorrhoids. So Allison is left high and dry while you rot in prison.'

The two men sat in silence. The wagon rattled and jolted on the rough road. They could hear the driver cursing his team of horses. It was stifling hot inside the closed wagon. Harry could make out three other shapes in the gloom.

'What about you, Mr Grant? I felt bad runnin' out on you but I couldn't allow you to take me in when I had Allison to look after.'

'Yeah, an' a fine job you made of that. If'n it's any consolation I asked my old man to look after her. He'll probably take her back to the Big G. How long you got?'

'Two years. Judge took into consideration my youth an' . . . anyways, you ain't tol' me about you.'

Harry sighed. Before answering he gingerly probed the top of his head. He could feel a large painful lump where the rifle barrel had bounced off his skull.

'I was railroaded,' he said at last. And then, because it had been all bottled up inside, he told Luke Parsons everything.

Because of his father's condition Harry had refrained from complaining when the old man visited him in the jail-house. The condition of his father had shocked him.

The shooting seemed to have knocked the stuffing out of the previously robust old man. Harry feared that his father would not last out his term in prison. So he had kept his complaints to himself. On each occasion he had reassured the old man that he would not be convicted on such a clear case of self-defence.

How naïve he had been. One by one the witnesses had come forward to testify. A picture had emerged of the Grants becoming drunk and causing trouble. They had picked on the stranger and insulted him. They had suddenly pulled out their guns and shot the man. He managed to get off a shot before being gunned down by Harry.

In spite of Harry's protestations the witness accounts had been allowed to stand. Harry had been convicted of unlawful killing. Because of his failing health and age his father was let off with a caution. Harry was sentenced to ten years. His father had pleaded for leniency. Because of his previous good character the judge reduced the sentence to six.

'Jeez, Mr Grant, didn't you have a lawyer or anythin' to defend you? I couldn't afford one. I don't know if'n it woulda made any difference.'

'Indeed, I had a shyster. He was supposed to be the best. My cousin hired him for me. He said it was the least he could do seein' as it happened in his saloon. But I might as well have had a common cowhand defendin' me.'

Harry sat in the gloom ruminating on the upheavals in his life.

'What the hell,' he shrugged, 'I'm here now and I'll just have to survive for the next six years. You'll be out afore me.'

'Look, Mr Grant, can we let bygones be bygones. I know I acted foolish joinin' up with my uncle. I didn't know he were a rustler.' He gave a rueful laugh. 'I was a bit of a greenhorn in this business. I came out here ahead of Allison intendin' to send for her when I had established myself. But she came out to look for me. Guess she got in trouble also. Honest to God, Mr Grant, in a way I was set up as much as you. When they tol' me they'd bought those steers and were to drive them to Mexico for to sell 'em for a profit I swallowed it hook, line and sinker. I was a mite suspicious but Uncle Bill kept joshin' me about known' nothin' about buyin' and sellin'. What do you say we try to get along without ill-feelin'?'

'Well, for a start stop callin' me Mr Grant.

Harry's the name.'

'Right, Harry. And thanks for takin' care of Allison for me. It sure makes me feel a lot better knowin' she'll be safe.'

'Pa'll look out for her. But it's Pa I'm worried about. He looked real sick.'

They both fell silent, each wrapped up in his own morbid thoughts. Harry again had a conscious vision of a beautiful young girl and the shock in her eyes when she saw the manacles on his wrists and ankles.

He was just a common killer as far as she was concerned. The story she would hear was of a barroom brawl and a fatal shooting. Closing his eyes he tried to block out the image but that limpid green gaze stared at him accusingly. He almost moaned aloud in his agony of mind. She was another man's woman. That man sat beside him on the way to the penitentiary. In some strange way he had become Harry's responsibility.

She obviously cared a lot for Luke. For that reason and that reason alone he would look out for the youngster by his side. He had no hopes of winning the girl for himself – the least he could do was look after the man she loved.

11

From the outside the house looked spacious and elegant. A broad porch ran along the front. The porch was equipped with comfortable-looking furniture. Well-stocked gardens surrounded the house and the whole area was bounded by a white picket-fence. A hired hand could be seen working among the beds. Everything looked well-tended.

Inside the house Richard Grant picked up a bunch of documents and crossed to the heavy iron safe. Kneeling down, he used a large key to open the thick reinforced door of the safe. He placed the documents inside the compartment and swung the heavy door closed. He moved back to the large desk, pulled out his gold hunter and consulted it. At that moment a woman came into the room.

She was a strikingly handsome woman. Long auburn hair hung in dark tresses to below her shoulders. Her large eyes were wide-spaced above a fine, straight nose. Full sensual lips gave hints of fire and passion smouldering within. Richard Grant turned and greeted his wife.

'Isabella,' he murmured and moved to embrace her. They kissed and held each other.

'I suppose you have to go into town this evening?

'Yes, dear. Some urgent business has come up. It needs my personal attention.'

'Have you forgotten I invited the Bishops and the Rogers over for cards this evening?'

'No, my darling, I haven't forgotten. It's just that this little matter requires me to be there. I'll be as quick as I can and I'm sure I'll make it back before the last few hands.'

He kissed her once more, straightened his clothing, took a derby from a hat-stand and waved her goodbye.

Arriving at the Hot Spur he entered the establishment from a door in the rear. As he emerged into the body of the saloon he looked around him. As usual at this time of the evening the place was crowded. He smiled with pleasure as he saw David Austin playing billiards with two strangers.

'Cousin David, you brought me some help, I see.'

David Austin was about to take a shot when Richard spoke. He turned and holding the cue across his chest smiled back at his cousin.

'Richard, how good to see you. Let me introduce you to two very capable men. This is Todd Bagot and Mott Green.'

Richard Grant looked at the two men. They were dressed in open-necked shirts and leather waistcoats. Both wore cartridge belts with holstered guns. Bagot was big and muscular. He had a square jaw that hadn't seen a razor in a week. Mean eyes stared back at him. Green was a big, burly man with a full, dark beard. He had the same mean eyes as his partner. Richard Grant nodded a greeting to the two men.

'I trust you men come with good credentials?'

The men said nothing. Their hard eyes said it all.

'Yessiree,' Austin said heartily. 'These are Texans, toughest breed on Gawd's earth.'

'I take it you brought more than two?'

For answer Austin used his cue to point towards a couple of tables. When Richard Grant looked to where his cousin indicated he noted a group of about a dozen men gathered around two tables. They were a tough-looking bunch – the sort of men that would cause merchants to lock up their stores along with their wives and daughters. Richard Grant nodded his satisfaction and turned back to David Austin.

'I trust you gave our dear cousin a fittin' send-off?'

'I did indeed. You would have been impressed by my melancholy manner. I told him fate had dealt him a bum hand. He was not aware I had an onion hid in my bandanna as I wished him farewell. My tears moved him most deeply. He bade me bear up as he expected to return in six years.

'After I left him I watched the prison wagon arrive. Big John was there, looking as happy as a coyote with a dose of buckshot up his ass.' The cousins burst out laughing. 'Mind, there was a gal with Uncle John. Pretty little filly she was. Never seen her before. Our Harry seemed a mite struck with her.'

'Harry and a pretty gal – naw, the only female he'd fancy'd be a broad-ass moo-cow.' Richard Grant laughed so hard he had to lean against the pool table. As the mirth diminished he noticed the new hands looking puzzled.

'My cousin, Harry Grant, has just been sentenced to six years in the penitentiary,' he explained to them. 'He killed a fella in the same trade as you gents. It's unfortunate for him but fortunate for me. He stands in the way of somethin' I want for myself. With him out of the way I can consolidate my position. You guys have come into my employ at just the right time. I'll have plenty of work for you if you ain't afraid of getting rough with a few of my...' he hesitated as if searching for the right term, '...competitors.'

Green gave a smirk. 'We git as mean as you tell us to. None of us is afraid to git bristly. However, if'n this cousin of yourn gits sent to the pen for a killin' is the same thing goin' to happen to us? That is, I reckon as you'll want a little shootin' done.'

'Friend Green, it don't work like that. I run this town. I own the freight yard, the livery, the general store, the bank, this establishment. Also I own the law. The sheriff knows who to arrest and who to leave well alone. I decide who gits hauled before the judge. You just do as you're told and leave the finer details to me.'

'Sounds a real dandy set-up you got here, Mr Grant,' Bagot interjected. 'Green and me'll serve you right well. All our men are mean sons of bitches reared on sour milk and sowbelly. Ain't nobody'll stand up to us if'n we tell them to lie down. Just you point us and we'll go like a pack of hound dogs after a bitch in heat.'

Green sniggered and a faint smile parted the dark beard of Bagot.

'Glad to hear it, Bagot. Now, you and your friends make yourselves at home. Tonight the drinks and entertainment are on the house. Mr Austin here will make all the arrangements for housin' and feedin' your bunch of bobcats.'

Touching their hat-brims the two lobos sauntered across to the hardcases awaiting them at the tables. Bagot spoke to them and received in reply a chorus of rebel yells. There was a concerted rush to the bar to take advantage of their new boss's generosity.

Richard Grant turned to David Austin.

'Let them enjoy themselves tonight. Tomorrow send them out to Parr's valley to clear out that den of nesters clutterin' up good grazin' land and not paying a cent for the privilege of livin' there.'

'I'll organize that all right. It'll be a good start for that bunch. See if they're as tough as they make out.'

'Do it then. I expect that valley to be cleared by the weekend.'

Richard Grant looked around him at the bustling saloon. Business looked to be pretty brisk, as it usually was. He made his way upstairs to his private suite of rooms. His intention was to cast an eye over the set of accounts for the saloon. Richard Grant trusted no one. By keeping a close eye on his business assets he forestalled anyone with a notion to swindle him. The few who had tried it in the past lay in unmarked graves out in boot hill.

No one took any notice of the dark-haired young man dressed in well-cut clothes walking into the Hot Spur. He was an extremely handsome young man with bushy black eyebrows that matched his generous black moustache drooping from his upper lip. Those alert eyes took in the scene, flicking around and noting details like stairs and exits. It was the habit of a lifetime of surviving in dangerous situations.

Ben North had been marshal of Toska for the last year or so. When he heard the news that his friend Harry Grant had been sent to the state penitentiary for murder he was perturbed as well as puzzled. Harry and he went back a long way. On at least one occasion he had owed his life to Harry Grant. Ben knew something stank in Lourdes when the news came to him. He left his deputies in charge and rode out. Harry Grant was his friend.

Ben North was in Lourdes to find out why a good man like Harry Grant was in the state prison.

12

Big John Grant sat on his veranda, his chair rocking gently. A girl sat on a cane-chair next to him. She looked very young and very beautiful. Her red hair framed a pale oval face. The old man and the girl were deep in conversation

'I notice you have a piano in your front room, Mr Grant. Do you play?'

'Naw, that was Harry's ma. She just loved that old machine. In the evenin' when all the chores were done she would play. Ain't bin played since she passed away.' The old man looked wistful. 'They were good days. Harry's aunts an' uncles an' cousins would arrive Saturday nights. Tom, he played the fiddle. This old house was a-hummin' with music and laughter. Good days, good days.'

'I play a little. Maybe you'd let me give you a tune sometime?'

Big John's face brightened.

'Sure would like that, Miss Allison.'

'Did Harry play at all?'

'Harry? Naw, he was more interested in

huntin' and fishin' and ridin'.' Big John laughed at the memory. 'Harry's aunts tried to git him interested. They gave up in the end. Said as he was a little savage – was no civilizin' him.'

'You're very fond of your son?'

A mistiness came to the old man's eyes.

'I love that boy – waal, he's a man now. I taught him to take care of hisself. Never thought to see him carted off to the penitentiary. I don't reckon I'll git to see him again. Six year is more'n I have left. That's why I took that trip into town to say goodbye. Damn near killed me. Doc he tol' me not to exert m'self. That ol' slug I took sure near about finished me. I ain't got much time left.'

'Surely you can visit.'

'Naw, I'm not fit for that trip. I'd only distress myself and wouldn't do Harry any good. He's a tough young'un. He'll survive.'

''Course he will. Though I'm not so sure if Luke will. He's not very strong, an' easy led.' The girl shook her head. 'I'll worry about him till I have him out again safe and sound.'

Big John reached out a gnarled hand and laid it on the girl's arm.

'If'n I know anythin' Harry'll look out for

him. Don't you worry about your Luke. He'll have a good friend in Harry.'

The girl frowned at the old man.

'Harry didn't tell you about Luke?'

'Tell me about him, what was there to tell? I reckon you and Luke was the pair he met on the trail. He said as he helped you some and then you rode on in the mornin'.'

'He didn't tell you any details...?'

Big John shook his head. 'Nope, just that what I said.'

The girl sat with her head bowed for a moment before speaking again.

'Luke and I come from Choriton. Luke decided to come out here and look up an uncle, Bill Tunsall. He said he would write to me when he was settled. I was supposed to come out and join him. He never wrote so I became worried and came on out here to look for him. When I got to Tuba I asked around for both Luke and Uncle Bill. A man called Irvine told me he knew old Bill well. I hired him and his buggy to take me to where he claimed he was. He insisted I needed bodyguards where we were going. I set out with these three men.

'They ... they had no intention of ... of keepin' me safe. They were settin' to rob me and do things to me...' her voice grew low and the old man had to lean close to hear her words. 'They pulled me off the wagon and ... and were attackin' me. I was fightin' them. God knows I was fightin' them but I knew I stood no chance. Then a miracle happened.' She raised her head and looked steadily at Big John. 'When all seemed lost a knight in shinin' armour came ridin' out of the blue and rescued me. I don't need to tell you it was your Harry.'

Big John slapped his knee. 'Gawddamn if'n that ain't our Harry. He never tol' me. He never tol' me. Gawdamn.'

'There's more, Mr Grant–'

'Stop calling me Mr Grant. Just call me John. Some call me Big John but I'm not so big any more. But carry on.'

'While Luke was with Uncle Bill they were stealin' cattle. Luke didn't know exactly what was goin' on. Bill told him they had bought the cattle and Luke had no reason to doubt him. Then Harry caught up with them. They tried to kill Harry but he managed to kill them instead. Luke was the only survivor. Harry was takin' him in when he rescued me. For some reason he left Luke and me alone and rode out to tend the herd. That was when Luke decided to make a run for it.'

Big John looked at the girl. It looked as if she were trying to tear her handkerchief in pieces.

'I ... I felt so bad ... after all that Harry had done for me...' She looked up at John and the big man saw the pain and regret in her eyes. 'Do you think Harry hates me? I suppose he thinks I was encouragin' those men who attacked me. It wasn't like that. I ... I ... oh, I hate myself...'

Big John said nothing. He just opened his arms and she came across to him. He felt her delicate body heaving as she sobbed.

'There, there, Allison dear. Our Harry won't hate you. He ain't the hatin' kind. He'll forgive you and he'll take care of Luke for you. So don't you fret yourself none. You don't know Harry like I do.'

The sound of hoof-beats sounded in the silence that grew between them. Allison quickly disentangled herself from the old man's comforting embrace and rubbed at her eyes with the long-suffering hankie. They turned to watch the lone rider come into the yard.

13

Ben North swung down from his saddle and walked the last few steps to the veranda. He tipped his hat to the young woman and nodded to the old man. Even though her eyes were red and swollen Ben noticed that the woman was very young and very beautiful.

'Howdy, folks. I'm lookin' for Mr John Grant.'

'Look no further, son. I'm Grant. What can I do for you?'

'I 'pologize about comin' at such a time. I heard about Harry, but that's what I'm here about. I'm a friend of Harry's. Name's Ben North.'

'Ben North, you're sure welcome. I heered our Harry speak about you. Any friend of Harry's a friend of mine. Step on up and grab yourself a seat. I was just about to order drinks. Will you join us?'

'I'd be mighty obliged, sir.'

One of the ranch hands came out and led the horse away. Big John's Indian house-servant brought a tray of drinks. When they were settled the old man and the girl waited for the visitor to state his business.

'I don't know what Harry told you about me. He's a good friend. Saved my life once.' The visitor paused for a reaction from his listeners.

'Gawdamn that boy,' Big John responded. 'He's as closed as a banker's vault.'

Ben North smiled at the old man.

'That's Harry, all right. Save your life and then fergit all about it. So you see, when I heard Harry was in trouble I had to come over and find out if'n I could help.'

'Too late now, son. Harry's in prison.' The old man sank back in his rocker, pain and sorrow etched in deep furrows on his face. 'It were all my fault too,' he muttered, 'all my fault...'

'Mr Grant, can you tell me what happened? I need to git a clear picture of the case.'

The old man sighed deeply. He took a long swig from his whiskey-glass, then proceeded to tell Ben North what had happened that fateful night in the Hot Spur.

'I was kinda drunk an' this fella kept pushin' and pushin'. Harry tried to calm me down but this fella was steamin' for trouble.

93

I went for my gun. After that I don't know much. I took this slug that'll be the death of me. Harry gunned the fella.' The old man looked sorrowfully into his glass. 'Now Harry's locked away for six years an' I'm sat here waitin' to die.'

Now it was Allison's turn to try and give comfort to the old man. She reached across and took his big paw in her dainty white hand. Ben North stared in fascination at the two so different hands locked together.

'Nonsense, John. You weren't to blame. The man was obviously lookin' for trouble. If it hadn't been you and Harry it would have been some other poor critter.'

But the old man could not be consoled. His pain-stricken eyes stared unseeingly into the distance.

'Mr Grant, this fella that was causin' the trouble – by any chance you know his name?'

The big man blinked, his attention slowly coming back to his guests.

'Name .. I reckon so. It came out at the trial. Name of Jonas Jones – a drifter by all accounts. No one knew anythin' about him.'

Ben North sat up straight in his chair, his eyes alight with some inner knowledge.

'You sure? – Jonas Jones, you said. Can

you describe him?'

Big John's tortured eyes stared at the young stranger.

'Describe him – he's branded into my memory like a hot iron on a steer. He were kinda shabby-like in dark clothin'. Almost like an out-of-work preacher. His face ... his face was like a ... a corpse – pale and narrow like. Wore gloves – I remember that. Damndest thing, seeing a man wearing gloves in a saloon.'

Slowly Ben North sat back in his chair.

'I'll be damned, Jonas Jones,' he murmured and to his listeners' frustration he fell into a contemplative silence.

'You ... you knowed this fella, Jones?' Big John asked at last.

'I sure do. He's a deadly assassin – or was, if'n you say Harry downed him. Gun for hire. Kill anyone for money – man, woman or child. Cold as a tombstone in a snowdrift. If'n you don't mind me speculatin', Mr Grant, someone wanted you dead. That's why Jonas Jones were in Lourdes. He was hired to kill you. It weren't your fault Harry's in prison. It's the fault of the person who hired him, Jones only killed for money.'

His listeners sat staring at him in dumbstruck silence. His words lightened something within Allison. She looked up hopefully at the lawman.

'There's someone in with Harry Grant. That also was a travesty of justice,' she said tentatively.

'Tell me about it, miss.'

After listening to her story Ben North took a sworn statement from her regarding the circumstances of Luke's conviction for theft.

'I'll do my best, Miss Allison. Seems to me a lot of injustice been goin' on. As upholder of the law it's my responsibility to put things right if'n I can.'

14

There were five of them – hard sinewy men. Lean and ragged, they were like hungry wolves and just as mean and unpredictable. Their victim wriggled and fought as calloused hands dragged him into the toilet block.

'I likes it when they struggle,' one of the men giggled.

'Sure as hell got some spunk,' another responded.

The youngster desperately twisted his head. As the hand clamped to his mouth shifted, he bit hard into the finger that slid into his mouth. With a foul oath the man jerked at his injured hand but the kid's teeth were clamped with remorseless determination.

'Gawdamn, git him off'n me!'

But his companions could not help. They were laughing fit to bust. It was slightly hysterical mirth. The men were stirred up with sexual tension and expectation. Their mirth was uncontrolled, as was their undue haste as they dragged the kid into the toilet area. The man with the bitten finger swore and was dragged helplessly in the wake of the captive.

A prison guard looked on, unconcerned, and wondered briefly whether he should join in the fun.

The victim certainly was a good-looking kid and young. Young and tender, he mused as the temptation to join in persisted. However he thought better of it when he contemplated the calibre of the men intent on molesting the youngster.

They were the hardest villains in a prison full of tough *hombres*. To join in the fun would mean setting down his carbine. Somehow he didn't think the pleasure of the kid's tender body would compensate for a hole in his head.

Inside the toilets, the hardcase with the bitten finger cuffed viciously at the kid's head. In the end the boy was forced to let go. The man stood back, blood dripping from his hand. He kicked the boy in the side. His victim tried to twist away but strong hands held him firm.

'Son of a bitch, I'm gonna kill that little varmint.'

'Gawdamn hell you won't, Jess. We'll keep

him for ourselves. An' he sure as hell won't die from what we'll give him. Make him a mite sore but we can use him as often as we want.'

'Git them britches of'n him.'

The struggles of the youngster grew more frantic as he twisted in the iron grip of his captors. He was helpless in face of the implacable disregard the men showed for his efforts. They shredded his clothing like vultures stripping flesh from a corpse. Buttons were ignored as the eager men tore at his shirt and pants.

'Flip him over.'

The men stared with slavering lust at the naked youngster stretched on the ground. Where his clothes had covered him his skin was white in contrast to his face and hands tanned by wind and sun. He was naked and vulnerable – a tender morsel for brutal men locked up for years with no hope of release.

'I'm first.' The man was undoing his pants while the other four each held an arm. With the hand removed from his mouth the boy screamed.

'No, you bastards. Don't do this. I ain't done nothin' to deserve this.'

'You was born, boy. That's what you done. You was born. We're your mother and father and brothers an' sisters now. We an' you's all family now. We gonna love you to death, boy. An' you gonna love us right back. Ain't that right, fellas?'

'Sure,' came back the chorus. 'We gonna love you to death.'

The boy opened his mouth to scream again but a wad of his torn shirt was shoved between his jaws.

'Jus' you lie there and think of me as your daddie.'

So intent were the men on their debauchery they failed to notice the movement by the door.

15

Harry Grant had been looking for his young rustler acquaintance when he heard the scream. His advance inside the toilets was silent. The first the men knew of his presence was when his boot connected with the man holding Luke's right leg. The man grunted and pitched forward against the man kneeling behind Luke.

'What the hell... !' he spluttered thinking his companion was trying to usurp his place. Then he realized his error as he saw Harry boot another of his friends in the side of the head.

'Gawdamned...' he screamed. He tried to rise but as his pants were around his ankles he was at some disadvantage.

The men Harry attacked were fast, vicious and dangerous. They had spent all their lives scavenging. Lying and stealing came naturally. All human life was there to be exploited. Compared to most men they were brute beasts. And they had the instincts of wild animals. Recovering rapidly they leapt to their feet and quickly closed with the attacker.

Harry back-pedalled, then suddenly swung a right cross at his nearest opponent. The fist smashed into the man's mouth but did not stop him. The man came on and closed with Harry. There was nothing for Harry to do but keep going back. Suddenly he crashed against the wall and the man was able to wrap his brawny arms around him. Harry brought his knee up and at the same time smashed his forehead into the man's nose. But these men were tough as wild boars and just as dangerous. For all Harry's efforts the man's arms stayed in place.

By now his companions were swarming around the two struggling men. Seeing help on its way the man who was entwined with Harry arched backwards and deliberately toppled to the floor. Struggle as he might Harry could not loosen the man's grip. A boot crashed into the side of his head and Harry saw stars.

Desperately he drove his forehead into the injured nose again. The man grunted and Harry struck once more, but not before a boot hit him in the kidneys. However, the grip around him loosened and the next kick flung him sideways and out of that crushing grip.

Harry rolled and rolled again but the brutal kicks kept landing. In desperation he grabbed at the nearest boot and heaved mightily. There was a yell as the boot's owner floundered and crashed heavily to the floor. The man Harry had head-butted was on his hands and knees shaking his head as blood streamed from a busted nose.

Somehow Harry was on his feet again. An attacker moved in and began swinging. Harry blocked and punched, blocked and punched. Blows were coming from all directions. Slowly he gave way, looking for an opening to deal a crippling blow. But the men he fought were tough *hombres,* used to rough-housing. They were slowly wearing him down.

Then the opening came. Swiftly he kicked and his boot slammed into a knee. There was a yell as the joint snapped and the man went down. Now there were three in front of him.

Harry was a mess. His body was a mass of aches and bruises where boots and fists had landed. Blood streamed from his nose and from a cut above his eye. He knew he could not last much longer at this pace. But his attackers were winded also. There was a pause in the frenzied action.

'You're daid, cowboy.' The man who spoke looked in as bad shape as Harry. 'Your grave's all ready fer you in this shit-house.'

Harry was breathing deeply, wondering whether maybe the speaker was right and that he wouldn't come out of the toilets alive. The wrestler who had been head-butted was back on his feet, his face a mask of blood and gore. Though he swayed un-steadily he was still a force to be reckoned with. Without warning his attackers surged forward.

Desperately Harry swung and punched. But more of his attackers' kicks and punches were getting through. He crashed back against a wall. The men closed in for the kill. Harry braced himself for the onslaught.

A fist pummelled his head and at the same time a boot came from nowhere and kicked him in the stomach. Harry grunted and went down. He knew this was the end.

Once on the floor the men would kick and stomp him to death. He had seen it before. Men gathering round a fallen victim kicking and stomping till the victim was either dead or injured so badly he never recovered. There was no mercy in these men. There was the bestial light of killing-lust in their faces as they closed in.

Harry curled himself into a ball, hoping to protect his head from the vicious kicking. The kicks rained down. Harry's body jerked as the boots thudded home. He was a mass of agony. Suddenly, as the outside attacker raised his boot to stomp, something solid and big hit him on the side of the head. He grunted and sagged against the wall. Harry saw movement beyond the attackers and looked up to see a naked form behind them. The youngster was wading into the hard-cases, swinging a large wooden bucket.

His attackers turned to fend off this new attack. For one man it was fatal. The bucket took him full in the face, smashing even further an already crushed nose. He screamed as he went down, the bones of his nose driving up into his brain.

It was Harry's chance. He was on his feet kicking and punching. Attacked from behind as well as in front the men broke and tried to flee. But the naked figure was demon-driven. A maniacal strength seemed to possess the slim form as he went about the business of wreaking as much damage as he could on his tormentors.

The bucket swung with the wild and vicious fury of the young man out for revenge. There was no defence against the wild swinging of the heavy object. Limbs, held up to fend off the blows, were smashed aside like twigs. The berserk youth ignored the few blows that managed to land on him. He was out for the kill. The bucket smashed into heads and faces.

With Harry on one side attacking with renewed fury and the savage bucket-wielder on the other side the men were being quickly beaten into submission. Even when the would-be rapists were on the floor the bucket rose and fell with unrestrained fury.

Harry blinked away the blood blinding his vision and saw the naked Luke battering the inert forms strewn around the toilet. A few were groaning while some made no movement at all even when the heavy wooden bucket smashed into their insentient forms. Harry staggered over to the boy.

'Luke, Luke, for gawd's sake...' The boy did not appear to hear him. The bucket rose and fell with unmitigated determination smashing heads and faces into bloodied pulp.

In desperation Harry grabbed the boy's hand.

'Luke. Luke, it finished – it's over!' The boy stared at him and slowly the light of madness faded. There was a thud as the bucket fell from his hands, sounding loud in the sudden silence as the frenzied action ceased.

'Harry, you. . . you all right?'

'Come on. Let's git outa here.'

At the doorway of the toilet they stopped and Harry looked cautiously into the yard. Out in the bright sun everything appeared normal. Prisoners slouched against the walls or sat in the dust, talking or playing cards or making up games with pebbles. He was aware of the nakedness of the youth beside him.

'Git your clothes. Pull them on.'

Luke did as he was bid. He was in a daze and Harry had to guide him. The garments were torn but Harry made the boy drape them around him as best he could. There was nothing he could do about the blood on his own face and hands.

'Just walk out easy. Make it slow, as if everythin's normal.'

The burning sun was a shock to their eyes after the dimness of the toilets. Harry tried to keep Luke on the side away from the guard. But he need not have worried. The guard hardly glanced at them as he continued to patrol. None of the guards on the watch-towers was interested in the two prisoners as they walked across the yard.

With a groan of pain Harry slumped to the ground with his back against the prison wall. Every bone and joint in his body throbbed in agony. He felt lightheaded. As he probed his nose he felt the bones grating together. He groaned again at the sudden pain. Luke swung his gaze to him, concern in his eyes.

'Gawdamn it, they bust my nose.'

Luke looked at his saviour. Harry's face was like a slab of raw beef. Eyes, nose and mouth were swollen to twice their size.

'Mr Grant, you look awful.'

Harry frowned at his companion. Even that slight movement hurt his face. The young man's unmarked face looked back at him with deep concern in his eyes.

'I s'pose you wish you'd never met me. I've been nothin' but bad luck for you. First I help steal your cattle, then I go on the lam when you was takin' me in and now this. Why'd you save me just now?'

And Harry wondered only briefly why he had gone to the rescue. But he knew the answer to that already. He could never stand by and ignore someone in trouble. Then he cursed inwardly as the picture of the beautiful young girl he had last seen standing in the road with tears in her eyes rose in his mind. He had promised her he would look after her beau.

Harry felt a great loneliness well up within him. He had never before seen a woman like Miss Allison and he knew he never would see the like of her again. When he got out of prison – that was, if he survived – she would be long gone. Her man Luke would have been released long before that and they would have departed to faraway pastures.

16

Ben North rode away from the Big G towards Lourdes. As he rode he planned his strategy. He always thought best when out riding. The horse could be left to follow the track while he put on his thinking-cap.

He had spent some time in the office of the Big G. There he had written to various officials. These letters had been given to one of the Big G's hands to carry to the nearest mail station. Now he was on his way to Lourdes in order to gather evidence to back up his misgiving regarding the trial of Harry Grant.

On arriving in Lourdes he stabled his horse. Then he had drifted around the town, casually talking to the gossips. Slowly he was building up a picture of a community that was able to railroad a man of previous good character. All indications pointed to one man, and that man owned the Hot Spur. That was where the fatal shooting of Jonas Jones had taken place, resulting in the conviction of Harry Grant for unlawful killing. Ben North eventually made his way to the saloon.

At that time of day the Hot Spur was comparatively quiet. It was the calm period before the evening entertainment began. As the night drew in, the crowds would cram into the saloon. The gaming-tables would open, the girls would circulate and the night's entertainment would be provided on the raised stage at the back of the hall.

The barman was happy to chatter to the good-looking young man, idly passing the time of day with beer and conversation. They talked about the weather, the state of politics and how many whores the barman had bedded in the Hot Spur. Eventually Ben turned the conversation around to the subject he was really interested in.

'Hear tell there was a shootin' in here a while back. You git many shoot-ups round here?'

'Naw, not that many.' The barkeep shook his head. 'You're thinkin', like as not, about Harry Grant killin' that drifter.' The man leaned confidentially towards Ben. 'I were here that night. Stood not more'n a few feet from them fellas.'

'Jeez, man, weren't you scairt with all that lead flying?'

'Me scairt? Hell no. I seen lots of shoot-in's. I weren't scairt. Stood there with my hand on the Peacemaker under the bar in case things got outta hand. Didn't need to use it. Sheriff Garrison were in there real quick and 'rested Harry Grant. I were eye-witness. Boss tol' me to testify. Even tol' me what to say. I done my duty. I were key eye-witness.'

'You was in court as witness? Jeez man, I ain't never bin in no court, never mind be no witness.' Which was a blatant lie for, as marshal of a big town, Ben North had operated in many a courtroom. 'What were it like?'

Ben could almost see the man's chest swell with importance as he gazed at his young inquisitor.

'I stood there and did my duty as an upright citizen. I weren't spooked by all them lawyers and officials. I took that there old oath on the Bible an' said my bit.'

'Jeez, what did you say?'

'I tol' it like it was, well tol' it like the boss tol' me what to say.'

'He tol' you! Why was that? Couldn't you remember?'

''Course I could remember.' The barkeep spoke as if he was talking to a simpleton.

'Mr Grant tol' me to say as Harry and Big John was proddin' that drifter into making a play for his gun. I was to say they was spoilin' for trouble. An' that's what I did.'

'But couldn't you have said that without bein' tol'?'

'You don't understand how courts works, do you?'

Ben shook his head. 'Nope, I sure don't.'

'Waal, it's like this, see. Mr Grant tol' me the good reputation of the saloon, not to mention the town, was at stake. If'n Harry Grant got off scot free fer that killin' then every villain for miles around would think Lourdes was a place outside the law. Then if' n that happened we'd be overflowed with trash. Respectable people would be forced to move out and Lourdes would become a lawless place not fitten fer decent folk to live in. He says as Harry would only git a light sentence but that'd send out the right message to troublemakers.' The barman smiled indulgently at the lawman. 'That's exactly what happened. Harry Grant got six year in prison and the town stays safe.'

Ben North nodded wisely as he took in this piece of artful manipulation.

'Sure 'nough I see it all now.' For a moment he toyed with his beer-glass. 'Say, seein' as how you've had all these whores I don't suppose you'll consider pointin' me in the way of a good-time girl whereas I'd git my money's worth?'

The barman laughed with genuine pleasure.

'Son, you sure came to the right man. Let me see now.' He frowned in concentration. 'Tell you what, if'n you meet me when I come off duty I'll be your guide.'

'Sure thing. My name's Ben. Where shall I meet you?'

'Pleased to be of service, Ben. I'm Toby. Why not meet me back at my place where'n we can freshen up somewhat an' have us a right ol' hellraisin' night.'

The lawman had to restrain himself from doing a jig of delight when he heard the barkeep's plan. It was better than anything he could have cooked up for what he had in mind.

True to his word Toby met Ben back at his shack on the edge of town. The barman was puzzled by the two horses tied up outside.

'What in tarnation you brung those nags for? It ain't but a step up the Street to the Hot Spur.'

'I kinda changed my mind about them whores, Toby. I thought instead we'd go for a little ride, you an' me. You see, I know a man would be interested in talkin' to you. He'd like as not want to hear all about your time in court, him bein' a judge an' all.'

'Gawdamn it Ben, I ain't goin' fer no ride this time o' night. Thar's these two gals 1 lined up awaitin' fer you an' me.'

In the dim silence of the night the sound of a gun being cocked came unmistakably loud to the ears of the barkeep.

'Sorry, Toby. You'll just have to keep your britches on tonight. You'll need them to keep your butt warm. We're riding to Toska.' Ben moved close and Toby felt something metallic against his wrists and a click as handcuffs locked in place. 'I'm the marshal over there an' I'm arresting you for pervertin' the course of justice.'

'Gawdamn you, I ain't goin' to no Toska.'

'Oh, you're goin' all right – either with a cracked skull, tied on that horse, or you can ride. You makes your choice.'

'You bastard. When Mr Grant hears about this your ass'll be fried.'

'Oh, he'll git to hear about it all right. I'll make damn sure of that.'

17

The horsemen swept out across the grasslands. They formed a small convoy with a two-horse buggy at the centre. Richard Grant drove the buggy. Beside him sat his strikingly beautiful wife, Isabella. She watched proudly as he urged the matched pair faster. Dust spurted up from the spinning wheels of the buggy. Her face was alive with excitement as the vehicle sped at breakneck speed along the track.

About a dozen riders accompanied the buggy, among them Bagot and Green with their band of hard-cases. The Big G buildings came in sight and the whole company piled into the yard of the ranch.

'Whoa, there! Whoa!' Richard Grant called out to the pair of horses as he expertly brought the buggy to a neat halt inside the yard of the Big G. The yard filled rapidly as his escort piled in behind him.

Richard Grant leapt nimbly from the buggy and turned with a wide smile to his lovely wife. She was laughing at him, flushed with the excitement of the fast drive out to the ranch.

'This fresh air agrees with you, my dear. You look enchanting,' he told her. With her sparkling eyes and raised colour she did indeed look dazzlingly beautiful.

'Flatterer, I bet you compliment all the women with your silver tongue.'

'No other woman compares in any way with you, my dear.' He held out his hand and assisted her to alight. As he turned to the house a rather beautiful red-haired girl appeared on the porch. She waited patiently for the new arrivals to approach.

'Howdy, miss,' Richard greeted her. 'I'm Richard Grant and this is my wife Isabella.'

The girl smiled and curtsied slightly.

'I'll fetch Mrs Dorothy. She's with Mr Grant at the moment. He's very low.'

Richard Grant frowned. 'We've come to visit our Uncle John. Aunt Dorothy is not our concern. Please take us to him.'

Before the girl could reply an older woman came into sight. Richard groaned inwardly.

'Aunt Dorothy,' he said with false heartiness, 'pleased to see you out and about. We've come to pay our regards to Uncle John. I believe he is unwell.' In sotto voce, he murmured to Isabella: *'I trust it's some-*

thing fatal for the old buzzard.' His charming smile belied his sentiments.

'When an old lion lies fatally wounded then the coyotes and vultures gather. I know what you are about, Richard Grant. You have pulled down a giant and penned his cub but you mark my words, a day of reckonin'll come. That cub may not be penned as securely as you would like to think and that same cub has claws – sharp claws.'

'Dearest aunt,' Richard spread his arms in exaggerated bewilderment, 'you talk in riddles. What's all this about lions and cubs? I have come merely to see my dyin' ... my sick uncle.'

'Ay, I know it will please you to know he is dyin'. Wishful thinkin' put the words in your mouth. He is dyin' of a broken heart and a bullet he took in the Hot Spur. Does it not strike you as odd that none of your uncles died a natural death? Is it not strange that their deaths benefit one member of our family – namely you...?'

Richard frowned deeply and put his hand thoughtfully to his lips before speaking.

'Do you know, Aunt Dorothy, that fact had totally escaped my attention. Now that you mention it, it does seem bizarre. I do hope it's not catchin'. I wouldn't like to think it would begin to affect the female line of the family.' His smile was bright and dangerous as he looked directly at the old woman.

Her smile was as bright and dangerous as his.

'You don't frighten me, nephew.'

Before she could continue the old Indian servant, Moss, appeared on the veranda.

'Come. Big John, he not good.' Dorothy immediately broke off and hurried inside. Richard turned to his crew who had waited patiently during his exchange with the old woman.

'Make yourselves at home, boys. It looks as if we won't have long to wait.'

The men dispersed towards the stables to care for their mounts.

'Well,' said Richard as he mounted the steps to the house and eyed Allison, 'and who have we here? Not a long-lost relation of old John come to watch him die and grab a slice of his ranch?'

Allison's face flushed with anger. She turned and fled into the house. Richard made a wry face towards his wife.

'I despair of this family. A poisoned-tongued witch for an aunt, a cranky old man for my uncle and a jailbird for a cousin. Now a rude young relation suddenly appears to complicate matters.' He directed Isabella to a seat before continuing, 'With a bit of luck the old man will soon join his brothers, wherever they might be.'

Almost as he finished speaking his aunt walked out into the veranda.

'Well, and how fares my dear old uncle?'

Dorothy looked at him with such a look of contempt that Richard, for all his *élan*, flushed with anger. With an effort he held his tongue.

'Your Uncle John is dead.'

'Ah well, the ripest fruit falls first. His time is spent.' Richard stood as he spoke and looked around him. 'It's fortunate I brought some of my men with me. They can take over the runnin' of the place for now.'

At that moment Allison came out onto the porch and moved to the side of the old woman. Her eyes were red and her face swollen with weeping.

'He was so kind to me,' she said, her voice trembling. 'I was a stranger and yet he treated me like I was his own daughter.'

Dorothy put an arm around the grieving girl.

'There, there, child. That was how he was. His heart was as big as a hay-barn.' She turned back to her nephew. 'What the hell do you mean, your men are runnin' the place? The Big G belongs to Harry now.'

'Yeah, yeah, old woman. But Harry is in prison, or didn't you know. Someone has to take charge – and who better than me? Someone needs to take care of Harry's interests.'

'Richard, I see now I was wrong about you...' his aunt began but was interrupted by Isabella. 'At last you see sense, Auntie, Richard has only the interests of his family at heart.' She stared sweetly up at the old woman. 'Richard just wants to take care of things till cousin Harry returns from prison.'

'As I was saying before I was interrupted by the bleating of a she-goat,' Dorothy continued acidly, 'at first I was inclined to refer to you and your henchmen as scavenging coyotes, but I see now I was wrong. You are more akin to maggots feasting on the dead bodies of your uncles.'

'Aunt, you have gone too far.' Richard's voice was tight with fury. 'When Uncle Tom met his unfortunate end I felt sorry for you and allowed you to stay on at his ranch, *my* ranch I might add, for Tom had borrowed heavily from my bank. Well, I–'

'How convenient it was to produce those notes after his death,' his aunt interrupted.

'Tom can't refute them from the grave. Is there no deed too low for you?'

'Enough, you old witch! I'll have you in court for bad-mouthin' me.' Richard Grant was white with the rage that consumed him as he faced his aunt. 'You be out of that house before Friday or I'll have you thrown out into the fields. I've had enough of your foul-tongued accusations. Out! I say, out! I never want to set eyes on you again.'

Allison was listening to this bitter exchange with wide-eyed consternation. Her eyes went from the proud old woman to the angry young man facing her. She watched as the woman drew herself up and disdainfully glared at her opponent.

'Too late, nephew.' Her voice was filled with contempt and barely controlled wrath. 'I've already bought a house in Lourdes. I could see this day coming. You had my husband murdered. So throwing an old woman out of her home would not cause you any remorse.'

Richard could take no more. He stepped forward, his face livid, and raised his buggy-whip. Allison gasped and instinctively stepped protectively in front of the old woman. Dorothy had not flinched during Richard's threatening movement.

Defiantly, Allison faced the raging man. For a moment the girl and the angry man stared eye to eye. Allison's manner was unafraid as she stood under the raised whip. Her lip was curled in scorn. Then a cool voice came from behind her.

'Step aside, Allison. I need room to shoot this mangy dog.'

With a quick intake of breath Allison swung round. She gaped as she saw the derringer in the old woman's hand.

'Oh God, no, Dorothy.' Allison now had her role reversed. She found herself in the process of protecting the man from the woman she had come to regard as her friend. 'Please Dorothy, this is not the way.'

Her hand reached out for the gun. For moments a battle of wills took place as the young girl out-stared the older woman. Dorothy's face was bloodless. Both women held on to the small gun – Dorothy with the butt in her hand and Allison holding the stubby barrel. Allison could feel the weapon trembling as passionate rages surged through the woman. An unholy light of madness lit the woman's eyes.

'I will send him to hell. There's a berth awaitin' him there.' She whispered fiercely, but Allison held her gaze.

'Please, Dorothy,' she said again. Slowly she could feel the rigidity ease in the woman's grip. The madness left her eyes and her shoulders slumped. Allison cautiously eased the gun from her grip. She slipped it into the pocket of her dress. Then the old woman was weeping. Allison wrapped her arms around her and held her close.

Footsteps sounded on the boards but she did not look around. Richard Grant and his beautiful wife pushed past the grieving women and entered the house of the Big G.

The old woman shuddered, then seemed to recover her former calm. She raised her hands and took Allison's face between them.

'Thank you, my child. The loss of all the men in my life has unhinged me. Grief batters at the walls of my sanity. Three senior members of the Grants have met a violent end. Big John is the last of that generation. Young Harry languishes in prison. He was my only hope to see justice done. Perhaps you should not have stopped me. But I suppose it is not my place to administer punishment for the crimes committed against this family.' She sighed deeply and drew a shuddering breath. 'We'll prepare Big John for burial and then leave this place. You'll come and live with me. Big John said Harry told him to care for you. I guess that obligation passes to me.'

18

The rifle butt hit the small of his back and he pitched out of the chair on to his face. He tried to curl his body away from the kick he knew would follow. The boot crashed into his ribs and a sharp agonizing pain tore into his chest. He gasped and his breath produced a splinter of pain in the area of his lungs.

His already battered body was a sea of agony. The face was swollen and bloodied. He could hardly see out of his eyes, so distended and discoloured was the flesh around them. His own aunt would not have recognized him if she had the misfortune to see him now in his present circumstances.

'So now, Harry, I will try once more. It's only because I like you that I am taking so much trouble with you.'

The prison governor was a large, chubby man. His hair was streaked with silver-grey lines. The hair was long and swept back in a carefully groomed wave. He smelt strongly of pomade. When he smiled strong, yellow teeth were exposed. He directed his toothy smile at Harry Grant.

'I'm a patient man, Harry.' The governor always called his charges by their first names. He maintained it made the inmates think more kindly of him.

'After all,' he would expostulate to those who cared to listen, 'these men are abandoned by society. They are cut off from their family and friends. When I address them by their first name they regain some semblance of their identity once more. They feel they are real people because of this. So they gain self-respect and act in a more responsible manner.' His theories were not borne out by results. Floggings, beatings and shootings by the brutal guards at the prison went on unabated.

Now he leaned back in his comfortable armchair, placed large fleshy hands over his paunch and eyed the prisoner in a fatherly manner.

The two guards behind Harry Grant bent forward and each gripped a shoulder. Grunting with the effort they hauled him back into his chair. Harry sat slumped in the seat. His head lolled on his neck. He had trouble staying upright.

'Right, Harry, let's start again. I don't

think you realize the seriousness of your situation. So I am giving you the chance to rethink it all.'

The effort to remain upright became too much for Harry. He slipped sideways. Brutal hands jerked him upright. He tried to focus on the man opposite. Waves of intolerable pain coursed through his body. He had been beaten so brutally he had lost consciousness on more than one occasion. Face-slapping and kicks brought him back again and again.

What did the fat man want? Harry couldn't remember. The fat man was speaking again. Harry tried to concentrate. The words hummed across the desk that separated him from the fat man. He saw the heavy spittoon near the desk. It was made from brass and tin. He began to focus on the spittoon. What was it about spittoons that he needed to know? Perhaps if he asked the fat man he could tell him? The fat man was talking.

'There has been a serious incident in my prison, Harry boy. I don't like things happenin' in my prison without my knowledge. Two men are dead and two so seriously injured they may never fully recover.

'They were discovered in the toilet block.

Shortly before they were found you were seen leavin' the area. The guard who saw you was certain there were other prisoners with you.' The governor paused and smiled benignly at the battered man slumped in the chair opposite. He couldn't be certain whether Harry Grant was able to hear him. Nevertheless he proceeded with his interrogation. 'That makes you the chief suspect. Having placed you at the scene of the crime I now need to know who else was involved.'

Harry's stubborn refusal to name names was the main reason for his brutal maltreatment by the fists and boots of the prison guards. Throughout the savage punishment he held on to the one thought. He had promised to protect Luke Parsons.

No one knew Luke had been involved in the fracas at the toilets. The guards had only noticed Harry. He had successfully shielded Luke from observation. Worried that his torn clothing would draw attention to him Harry had sheltered the younger man with his own large frame. The ploy had been successful and that was why Harry was now being interrogated.

The governor was in charge. He must be seen to control all aspects of prison life. Therefore all infringements of prison rules were ruthlessly punished.

'Now, Harry, once again I am askin'. Who helped you murder those men in the toilets? I know you're in here for murder. But you had to have help to inflict such injuries on those men. So who was with you?'

Harry remembered now. Through the fog of pain he remembered what he mustn't reveal. A vision floated into his mind.

At first it was a flash of long, fair-skinned legs and the gentle swelling of white breasts. The image slowly resolved into a pale oval face. For the first time he noticed the freckles splattered across the nose. Green eyes gazed anxiously into his.

'I'm worried...' she had said. What was it she was worried about? And the answer came – the rustler. She was worried about the rustler. And he had promised to look after him. That was what he could not speak. He could not reveal the name of the man involved in the attack at the toilet block.

The word of Harry Grant was binding. He could not break that faith no matter what the cost. And so he endured the beating and wished he could pass into unconsciousness again.

He focused on the spittoon. There was

something he knew about spittoons – something important. He tried to concentrate. While he looked at the spittoon through pain-misted eyes the governor kept talking patiently to him.

'I might be inclined to go lenient on you, Harry, if you agree to co-operate. I could lighten your punishment. You will have to be punished, Harry. Murder is a serious crime even inside a prison. The rule of law operates in here just as it does outside. It will be my painful duty to administer that punishment. But it is not unknown for me to be lenient. Now, Harry, once more I am asking. Who was with you in the toilets? Who helped you beat those men to death?'

The spittoon – Harry remembered about spittoons. Some were manufactured with a weighted base to lessen the likelihood of their overturning. Sometimes lead was used and sometimes sand was poured into a cavity. Harry stared at the spittoon. That was it! The base would be heavy. Now he had to concentrate as he tried to remember why that was important. He felt a blow to the back of his skull as one of the guards cuffed him.

'Answer the boss when he talks to you.'

Harry's throat was dry. He opened his

mouth to speak but only croaked. With his finger he pointed to his mouth. His lips were split and discoloured – his mouth filled with blood. Just the effort to open his mouth was painful. In front of him on the governor's desk was a heavy cut-glass decanter on a tray with matching tumblers. It was filled with an amber liquid. Harry pointed to the decanter and then again at his mouth.

'Drink...' he croaked.

The governor nodded to one of the guards. Instead of using the decanter on the desk the guard went to a bucket standing in a corner of the room. He brought a dipper of water to the prisoner. Harry reached for the dipper. The guard teased him and kept pulling back out of reach.

'All right, Fred, that's enough. Give him a drink.'

Harry noticed that his hands were trembling when he took the dipper. He managed to get the water to his mouth. It might have been urine for all he knew but he slurped at the liquid. His throat was swollen and dried and he had difficulty swallowing. He was fascinated by the tremor in his limbs. The dipper rattled against his teeth. Suddenly the dipper was wrenched from his lips. The guard slung it across the room and it clanged against the bucket.

Harry was reminded of the bucket swinging in the toilets. He remembered the solid clunk of the wood against heads and limbs as Luke battered his attackers.

Damn the kid, but he had pluck. Harry would be the one lying in the morgue if the rustler had not come to the rescue. Harry had no illusions about his probable fate as the prisoners gathered round viciously kicking their helpless victim.

'No one helped me do nothin'.' His voice was a croak – the words hardly audible. 'I didn't do nothin'…'

He had not the ability to tense himself against the expected slug. The blow came each time he gave that answer: *I didn't do nothin'*.

Helplessly he pitched out of the chair. This time he went further forward. The guards had to come around his chair this time to pick him up.

They were becoming bored now. No matter how vigorously they hit this stubborn hardass he still gave the same stupid answers. Normally a prisoner at this stage of the proceedings would be willing to say anything to stop the beating.

The guards were experts in barbaric interrogation. They vied with each other in the brutal treatment of their charges. The prisoners walked in constant fear of drawing attention to themselves. A guard would beat a prisoner for just looking at him. They just couldn't understand how this hardass cowboy could take so much punishment and not break under it. When Harry moved it caught them completely off guard.

The spittoon came round in an arc. It did have a weighted bottom. There was a satisfying clunk as it hit the guard in the side of the head. Spittle sloshed from the container and splashed on to Harry's clothes. With a startled cry the guard fell sideways and stumbled into his companion.

Harry was scrabbling around on hands and knees. His mangled fingers found the stock of the rifle dropped by the guard when the spittoon hit him. In spite of the pain it caused he gripped the barrel of the weapon. He drove the stock into the kneecap nearest him. There was another scream and the guards went down in a tangle. They were not used to prisoners fighting back. Their speciality was beating helpless men who could not retaliate. Now this cowboy, who should have been beaten into submission, had taken the initiative and was fighting back.

Cradling the rifle Harry rolled sideways and then came up on to his knees. He fumbled with the weapon. Crushed fingers were not much use for operating the intricate mechanism of a rifle. He had to get a shell into the breech – had to hold the guards at bay and escape from this hell-hole. Harry was working on instinct only. The compelling need for survival was uppermost. He would kill his tormentors if necessary.

Harry came from sturdy stock. His ancestors had trekked thousands of miles across the plains of America, carrying all they possessed in their wagons. The covered wagon was their home. It was a brutal existence. They survived sickness and disease, Indian attacks, snake-bites, heat, drought and floods. And they endured. The hardy among them survived – the weak went to the wall.

The trail west was dotted with the graves of those without the stamina to survive. Only the hardiest of the breed survived. They built places in which to live and work, from the materials they found at hand. Log-cabins or sod-houses and even caves became home to these pioneers. Quitters did just that – quit – and did not make it.

Harry Grant was no quitter. He fumbled with the mechanics of the gun in his torn hands. The two terrified guards scrambled for the exit. Their Nemesis had arrived. No more was it fun to batter a helpless prisoner. This one was fighting back. The guards fought to get through the doorway.

The governor of Willoughby Penitentiary may have been a benign-looking man. He had been governor for ten years. When he had taken on the job the prison had a bad reputation. His outer layer of softness hid the hardness that was the core of the man. A man did not get to be governor of a prison without a streak of toughness and cruelty. He tamed the prison and stayed in the job. Also, for a big man he could move very fast.

Harry sensed rather than saw the movement behind him. By now his torn and bleeding fingers had manipulated the loading mechanism. He brought the rifle round and fired instinctively. The big man flinched as the bullet cut away the lobe of one ear. As he had stood he had swept up the decanter of whiskey. This he now flung into the prisoner's face. The heavy glass container hit Harry on the forehead and he fell back. The pungent smell of spilt spirits was strangely reviving.

Frantically he worked at the rifle for another shot, his damaged fingers not operating very efficiently. By now the governor was around the desk. He ignored the blood streaming from his torn ear. This worm scrabbling round on the floor needed stamping on and he was the very man to do it. He ignored the rifle in the prisoner's hands. His boot lashed out and caught Harry on the side of the head.

The blow with the heavy decanter had dazed an already befuddled Harry. He had endured the beating in the toilets followed almost directly by the brutal interrogation by the prison guards. Harry was functioning on adrenaline only. All his reserves had been used up. The vicious kick on the side of the head exploded a kaleidoscope of colours inside his skull. Harry Grant toppled sideways as a wave of blackness took over from the explosion of colours. He did not feel the next kick, or the next one or the one after that.

19

The prison was buzzing with suppressed excitement. Whenever they could the prisoners gathered in little groups and discussed the signs. Those in the know had seen a prisoner being taken to the governor's office. After a while a shot had been heard. What happened while the prisoner was there was shrouded in mystery. Those in charge of the morgue and dispensary had waited for a wounded man to be brought in.

'More'n likely they'll bring in the body. Those bastards only shoot to kill. Don't know no other way.'

Instead the governor had arrived in the dispensary needing medical attention for an injured ear.

'Goddamn cut m'self shaving,' he grumbled – his louring stare daring the attendants to contradict him.

The wound had bled profusely, requiring all the skills of the inexperienced medical staff to stanch it. A bulky bandage now adorned the governor's head.

In a vain attempt to disguise the unsightly dressing the governor had perched a large Stetson on his head. With this headpiece the wounded man looked even more massive. The prisoners gazed at him with awe but no one dared to laugh. The sight of that grim face beneath the quaint headgear spelt trouble for someone.

The nature of the governor's wound was avidly discussed.

'Gawdamn earlobe missin'.'

'I hear the whole ear was gone.'

'Cut hisself shavin' he says.'

'Must'a bin usin' a gawdamn Bowie knife.'

Then came the order next morning for a general assembly. The prisoners gathered in the main exercise yard. The full company of guards was on parade all fully armed. Speculation was rife. The prisoners glanced up at the sentries posted around the walls. They were all facing inwards towards the yard. The guard towers were also heavily manned.

The prisoners avidly watched the preparations proceed. A table was carried into the yard. Then a couple of chairs were arranged around this. Decanters and glasses were placed upon the table. A bowl of fruit appeared. The prisoners watched, their mouths watering as the food and drink was produced. They would have traded an arm or a leg to be a guest at the table of honour.

After everyone had been hanging round for some time with nothing much happening the governor himself appeared. He was flanked by two guards, both heavily armed with sidearms and carbines. With great deliberation the governor seated himself at the table. When he was seated to his satisfaction he poured a drink. Prisoners licked their lips as they watched. Sipping the liquor the governor nodded in satisfaction. He turned and spoke to his escort. The man made a sign to someone out of sight.

There was a disturbance to one side. All heads craned to see what was happening. A man was being led out between two guards. Rather, he was being dragged out for he looked as if he was not able to walk under his own steam.

He slumped in the grip of the men on either side of him barely moving his legs as he was bundled along. His face had been battered beyond recognition. If his head had been dropped on to the table at which the governor sat, it might easily have been mistaken for a raw slab of beef set there prior to roasting.

A collective sigh went up from the assembled prisoners. The guards dragging the miscreant had stopped by Lot's wife. Now at last, they knew what was to happen.

Set firmly in the tramped-down dirt of the yard was a thick post. Hewn from a large tree-trunk a man could just about embrace its girth. So solidly was it set in the earth that it was easy to imagine it might have been there before the prison was built.

As far as the prisoners were concerned the post was known affectionately as Lot's wife. The Biblical connotation might have been lost on most of the prisoners. Lot's wife had been transformed into a pillar of salt. The men who copulated with Lot's wife writhed not in ecstasy but in agony. The salt was rubbed into the raw wheals on their backs. For Lot's wife was the prison's whipping column.

The crowd in the yard watched avidly as the guards tugged the prisoner's arms up around the post. Above head-height were two iron rings hammered into the wood. Once secured to these the victim could only twist helplessly against his constraints as punishment was administered.

The guards stepped back. Two fresh men strode forward. They were stripped to the waist. Exertion in the hot sun was sweaty work. Each carried a long flexible leather whip. They popped the whips experimentally then turned and looked towards the governor's table.

The governor had risen to his feet and was walking towards the whipping-pole. He looked big and formidable, his clothes stretched tight on his fleshy body.

'Well, my friend, you have had a night on which to ponder your plight. I'm going to have you flogged. The number of lashes you'll receive depends on your answers to my questions. They're the same questions as before. Who were your accomplices? Name them and you don't get as many stripes.'

The bound man did not respond. His shirt had been removed. As he hung from the iron rings cords of muscle rippled like live snakes across his arms and shoulders. Dark bruises had mushroomed on his fair skin. His once-long blond hair had been shorn short. The handsome face that had characterized Harry Grant was no longer recognizable. Blood and bruises had obliterated the features.

The governor nodded. He had not expected the man to break. Anyone who, after the brutal beating he had received at the hands of his guards could still take a rifle away from them was one tough *hombre*. It would take the flogging to break him. The governor smacked his lips in anticipation. The punishment promised to be a long and painful process. He did not expect his prisoner to survive. So much the better.

'Listen up, you scumbags,' he suddenly shouted out to the assembly. 'This man is guilty of a crime. He committed murder in my prison.' He paused for this to sink in. 'Some of you helped him. I want to know who you are.' He jerked a thumb at the tethered man. 'This son of a bitch won't tell me. I'm dependin' on you to come forward and identify yourselves.' He looked around at the mass of humanity already beginning to sweat as the sun grew higher in the sky. 'If you own up now your punishment won't be so harsh. But if'n I have to find out the hard way – and find out I will, I always do – then you too will be ruttin' with Lot's wife.'

The silence grew in the yard as the governor waited. At last he walked back to his table, sat and poured a drink.

'Proceed with the prisoner's punishment.'

The guards appointed to administer the flogging took a stance each side of the prisoner. They rotated their shoulders and took in deep breaths. Before they could begin there was a commotion at the gates of the prison.

Heads craned to see what was causing the interruption of the entertainment. A smartly turned-out young man somewhat travel-stained strolled inside. He was escorted to the table and presented to the governor. A marshal's badge gleamed on his well-cut coat.

'Howdy, Governor, I'm Marshal Ben North.' He laid a document wallet on the table. 'I have release documents for two prisoners held here.'

The governor smiled up at the young law-man.

'Welcome, Marshal. You timed it just right. I have a show laid on. Set yourself down and pour yourself a drink. The show is about to start.'

He picked up the wallet and opened it. For some minutes he studied it. Carefully he folded the papers back into the leather wallet.

'Cain't stop the proceedin's just now, Marshal. We'll tend to this after.'

He turned and motioned to the floggers.

'Proceed,' he called out.

The crack of leather on flesh snapped out across the prison yard.

20

Ben had witnessed many things in his career as marshal but he had never witnessed a flogging. Somehow he did not think he was going to enjoy the experience but what the hell. Another hour to humour this fat man and then he would retrieve his prisoners and be on his way. Though the sooner he was clear of this hell-hole the better.

Ben knew when to be patient. He did not want to rile the governor by being in too much of a hurry. The man was obviously set to enjoy his entertainment, as he called it. For Ben, whipping a helpless man, no matter what his crime, was not his idea of entertainment.

The whip-masters worked steadily. Each time the lash landed there was an audible crack. At first the whips raised red wheals like scarlet serpents writhing across the prisoner's back. As the men got into their stride and began to enjoy their work ribbons of blood erupted. Eventually the skin began to break up as the leather throngs bit into the soft flesh.

Ben tried to look away but found his gaze coming back to the raw flesh being slowly exposed by the brutal lashing. He marvelled at the man's stoicism. Only once did he break his silence. The floggers stopped and bent close to listen to something the man had to say. After a moment they turned in the direction of the governor and lifting their hands wide shrugged expressively. The governor responded with a pointed finger and a nod. The scourging continued.

No longer did the man tethered to the whippingpost stand of his own volition. He sagged against the thick pillar, held upright by the throngs binding him to the rings set high into the wood. Ben North wondered how a human could take such brutal punishment and still live. He slid a covert glance at his host.

The fleshy face was wet with sweat in spite of the man's efforts to mop at it with a large bandanna. His coarse lips were gaping open with excitement. The eyes under the heavy brows glittered with callous enjoyment. Where Ben North found this exhibition of brutality nauseating it was obvious his host found the performance exhilarating.

Ben looked away and found himself

staring into the clear blue sky. He did not think it could get much hotter. But then again it was only mid-morning. Towards midday he feared temperatures would soar even higher.

The crack of the lash on raw flesh continued unabated. He tried to shut out the sickening image of the man on the end of the harsh punishment. Then he noticed the dots circling in the simmering heat.

For long moments he watched the birds floating effortlessly on the spirals of hot air. Strange how these omens of death had senses far beyond human understanding. A helpless creature being beaten to death was a magnet for these scavengers. Then a sudden disturbance in the yard distracted him from the vultures circling above the prison.

A prisoner was standing alone in the yard. Ben noted his youth – no more than a boy.

'Cut him down ... stop it!' His cries had the desired effect. The guards with the whips stopped their efforts and stared at the youth.

'Harry didn't do nothin'. It was me! I did it ... I did it! I beat the men. Harry wasn't even there.'

Ben North sat up in his chair and in spite

of the heat a cold sweat broke on him. Harry – the name drove like a rivet of hardwood into his brain. Harry! Then he was running across the yard.

The body hung from the post like a side of beef in a slaughterer's yard. Blood had run down and made dark stains on the man's trousers. He reached the bloodied carcass, brushing past the sweating men whose whips now hung idly. Gently he moved the head around to view the face. The bruised and battered face almost matched in texture the ruined back. In spite of the damage Ben North recognized the man who hung from the punishment-post. Almost without thinking his knife was out and the sharp blade sliced through the thongs. The body sagged into his arms and Ben North almost broke down.

'Harry ... Harry ... it's me, Ben. I've come to take you home.'

'Damn your hide, Marshal, what the hell do you mean interferin'. Git away from that prisoner.'

Carefully Ben North laid the body of his friend against the wooden post. His actions were gentle as he handled the mutilated frame. That done he moved with the speed of a striking rattler. No one saw the movement of his hand as he drew his Colt. It was only one quick step to the fat man with the bandaged head. The governor grunted as the barrel of Ben's colt rammed into the softness of his gut.

'You knew this was the man I'd come to release. Yet you still had him flogged.' The voice was low and tense and the big men heard the anger in it.

'Marshal, you're exceedin' your duty. This prison is in my jurisdiction. If'n you don't take that pistol away now I'll order my guards to shoot.'

Ben smiled thinly as he stared into the face of the governor. The man saw the anger in those eyes. It was not hot anger, it was an icy-cold fire that burned there. Not many men had seen those eyes in that state and lived to talk about it. For the first time in his life the fat man felt fear.

'I won't make the mistake of killin' you outright, fatso. I'll gut-shoot you or put one in your spine.' The words were spoken in a chilling, matter-of-fact tone. The fear in the fat man spread. 'I'm leavin' this hell-house and I'm taking this man with me. If'n he dies on me I'll come back for you. That is, providin' I ain't killed you already. Now, we can do this easy or hard. Don't bother me either way.'

The governor looked into those ice-laced eyes and a quaking began in his guts. He licked his suddenly dry lips.

'What you want me to do?'

'You tell your guards not to interfere. Harry Grant has received a free pardon from the state and is a free man. They harness a wagon and team, they puts a mattress in and then they load the prisoner.'

'Cain't you take that pistol out of my guts? It's mighty uncomfortable.'

'If'n it goes off it'll be even more uncomfortable.'

Marshal Ben North waited. He had sized up his opponent. The man was a bully and probably a coward into the bargain.

'Git a wagon, you men. The marshal's leavin' with the prisoner.'

As Ben watched the guards scurry to carry out the governor's orders he noticed the youth standing uncertainly in the middle of the yard. On a sudden hunch he called out.

'You there. What's your name?'

'Luke Parsons, sir.'

Ben gave a thin smile. 'Luke Parsons, this is your lucky day. I have pardons here for two men. Harry Grant is one and Luke Parsons is the other. Git your things and help the guards load Harry. Make sure they's gentle with him. My hands are pretty full at the moment.'

The youth came at a run.

'I ain't got no things.' He knelt by the recumbent body of Harry Grant. 'He's ... he's not daid...?'

'For the governor's sake I sure as hell hope not.'

'You realize this is agin' all regulations.' The fat man's voice quavered as he spoke. 'Just put away that gun and I'll assist you any way I can.'

'Sure, sure. I believe you. When I gave you those pardons you could have told me it was Harry Grant hangin' on that pole. Instead you about killed him. I'm takin' no chances with a snake like you. This gun stays where it is. Just you pray you don't agitate me none. It's takin' all my control not to pull this trigger an' to hell with the consequences.'

'Damn you, I'll have a warrant sworn for your arrest as soon as you leave here. No one comes in my prison and treats me like a common felon.'

The governor sucked in his breath. If he thought his threat would have any effect the notion was dispelled by the extra pressure the marshal put on the pistol pressing into his abdomen.

'Keep talkin' like that, Governor. It frightens me som'at. When I gits scared I starts shootin' ... reflex action, I guess.'

The governor opened his mouth and then on second thoughts closed it.

The wagon creaked to a stop beside the little group. Luke supervised the loading of the unconscious Harry. When all was ready he looked at the two men pressed so close together and waited for instructions.

'You drive a team?' the marshal asked.

Luke nodded. 'Of course.'

'Git the gates open and take her out.' The marshal turned to his hostage. 'Come friend, time for a little walk.'

The whole prison was on hand to witness the newcomer escort two prisoners and their governor through the gates. The wagon led, then came Ben North on his saddle horse. Alongside the marshal's mount stumbled a sweating, cursing governor. Around the fat man's neck Ben had tied one of the blood-soaked whips that had lashed his friend to ribbons. They were several miles down the road before he released the quivering, raging man.

'When we meet again you better have a

gun in your hand.'

'When we meet, you son of a bitch, I'll have a warrant for your arrest,' gasped the governor. 'Then, by gawd, I'll have you in my prison. You'll wish you'd never met me. In fact you'll wish you'd never been born.'

The marshal reached into his belt and brought out his knife. His captive shrunk back and in spite of the heat, paled visibly as the marshal leaned over towards him. The blade sliced through the leather throng of the whip. Ben North tossed the useless scourge to the dust of the trail. Without another word he turned and nudged his horse forward.

Behind him on the trail the governor stood and cursed. The sound of the curses faded as the wagon and rider drew further and further away.

'Where to now, Marshal?' Luke Parsons asked.

'I had reckoned on headin' for the Big G. I promised Big John I'd bring his son home. That was afore all this happened. Somehow I don't think Harry's in a fit state for such a long haul. There's a town about twenty mile. We'll head there. Try and git Harry fixed up. Gawdamn that governor to hell! Why was he floggin' Harry, anyways?'

'Should've been me hangin' on that post,' Luke said. He went on to tell the marshal of the attack in the toilets. 'I didn't know they was goin' to flog Harry till they brought him out. When I realized what they were doin' I knew Mr Grant wouldn't spill my name. I ... I was scared to speak out afore...' His voice dropped almost to a whisper. Ben North had to lean in close to hear the words above the rumble of wheels and the creaking of the wagon. 'He saved my life...'

Ben saw tears spilling down the boy's cheeks. For a few moments they rode in silence. Above them the sun burned fiercely down on them. The dust on the trail hung on the air for a while after they passed, then settled again, leaving no trace of their passing. After a while Ben spoke.

'That was a mighty brave thing you did back there steppin' out like that for Harry. He'da been proud of you.'

'I left it too late... I was too scairt... He saved me an' I was too afraid to help him...'

'Don't beat yourself up, boy. You did good. When that snake had finished floggin' Harry he'da hung you out there and give you the same treatment. You saved him when you shouted out Harry's name. Up till then I didn't know it was Harry. I'm as much to blame as anyone.'

They rode on in silence, lost in their own thoughts. At last Ben North spoke.

'When we git Harry settled you'll have to light out for the Big G. Tell Big John what's happened. He'll send help. I don't trust that governor. Son of a bitch might just try to git even. I'll stand guard on Harry till you brings help.'

The wagon carrying the injured man trundled on. Jolted about on the mattress Harry Grant slipped in and out of consciousness. He had no idea where he was or what had happened to him. His body floated in a sea of fire. He wasn't sure if he was alive or dead.

21

The new straw-boss of the Big G strolled out on to the veranda with a steaming mug of coffee in one hand and a lit cigarette in the other. He sat on one of the cane-chairs and puffed contentedly at his smoke and sipped his coffee. Todd Bagot considered he was one lucky son of a gun.

After years of earning a precarious living as a hired gun his fortunes had changed on his meeting David Austin. That worthy had persuaded Bagot to up stakes and follow him to Lourdes. There he had met Richard Grant. That introduction had changed his life dramatically. Now Grant had made him boss of the biggest cattle ranch in the region.

Working the ranch for him were thirty hands. On top of that he had a dozen of his own gunnies directly answerable to him. They were his insurance in case anything went wrong with the present arrangements.

His thoughts were interrupted as his breakfast arrived. The old Indian houseboy placed a plate of fried food before him and turned to go.

'Bring fresh coffee, you useless piece of horse-dung,' Bagot called after him. 'Gawdamn Injun, I'll git rid of him and git me a young filly to tend me.' Cheered by this thought Bagot fell to eating.

Back in the kitchen the old Indian picked up a mug. He hawked heartily and spat into it. Thoughtfully he swirled the spit around. Placing a finger over one nostril and holding the mug in position he added the contents of his nose to the mix. Satisfied with this concoction he poured steaming coffee from the pot on the stove into the mug. Thoughtfully he stirred molasses into the coffee before delivering the mug to his new boss.

'Yore mother was a whore and your father a prairie-dog,' Todd Bagot cheerfully informed the house-servant. He slurped from the coffee-mug as the old Indian began to clear the table. 'But you sure make damn good coffee.' The servant disappeared soundlessly inside. 'Gawdamn, slimy Injun gives me the creeps.' At that moment he saw the rider approaching. Bagot loosened the gun in his holster. He never went anywhere without a sidearm.

The mounted man had obviously ridden far. His horse was plodding wearily the last few hundred yards to the ranch. Bagot watched suspiciously as the dust-covered rider pulled up near the veranda and slid off his mount. He relaxed somewhat as he noted the extreme youth of the newcomer.

'Yeah, stranger, you looking for a job?'

'No sir, I'm wantin' to speak to Mr Grant, Big John Grant.'

Bagot's eyes narrowed somewhat.

'What's your business with Big John?'

Luke hesitated before replying. In the short time he had been in the territory the youth had been tricked into helping his uncle rustle cattle – then he had been falsely imprisoned for horse-stealing. On top of that he had witnessed the brutish behaviour of the prisoners and those in charge inside the penitentiary. It was an older and wiser Luke Parsons who stood in the yard of the Big G. There was no way he was going to reveal his business to this big, unfriendly man.

'Its kinda personal. I gotta speak to Big John himself.'

'That's OK kid, I'm straw-boss round here now, so you kin tell me.'

Luke took his hat off and wiped his sweating brow. He thought it strange the foreman did not offer him hospitality.

'Sorry, mister, I can only speak to Mr Grant. It's real personal-like.'

Tired of the conversation Todd Bagot pointed out beyond the pasture.

'See that big willow tree? If'n you want Big John he's out there.'

Luke looked out to where the man was pointing. He could see nothing to indicate that anyone was around.

'Thanks. With your permission I'd like to water my horse and then mosey on over there.'

Bagot pointed to the water-trough near the barn and sat down, effectively dismissing the youth. Luke watered his beast and splashed his own face. He had smelt the coffee. Most places would have offered some hospitality. Luke had sensed the hostility in the man. He would just have to see Harry's father and get the help they needed. Strange that the Big G would hire such a surly man as boss. He pointed the mount in the direction of the willow.

As he approached the tree he could see a figure seated beneath it. Closer up he discerned it to be an Indian. Nothing in all he had heard about Harry Grant's dad had indicated him to be an Indian. Then he saw the headstones. He nodded to the squatting figure and dismounted. Before he read the lettering he suspected what he would find.

'Big John he go die last week.'

'Gawd rest his soul,' the youth endorsed, as he turned to the old Indian.

'What's happenin' here? I need to find help for someone. I was told Big John would give me that help. But that fella up at the ranch didn't seem very friendly.'

The Indian studied the boy for some moments.

'It Master Harry?'

Luke sighed. He had to trust someone. He nodded.

'Master Harry hurt bad. He needs someone to care for him. I was sent here to bring help. What's goin' on?'

'Come. I take you to Miss Dorothy. She know what do.'

The old man circled around the barns and brought the boy to the rear of the ranch house. Luke almost fell off the horse when he stopped. The Indian looked shrewdly at the boy.

'You have breakfast, then I take you.'

He led the way into the kitchen and quickly served up a heaped plate of grub to his guest.

Todd Bagot was next door getting ready to

ride out on the day's business when he heard the voices. He had observed the Indian with the boy at the grave. His suspicions roused, he crept to the doorway and listened.

As Luke ate he talked. He told the Indian about Harry's condition. Bagot heard enough. He knew sufficient of Richard Grant's plans to know the safe return of Big John's son was not good news. Soundlessly he retreated and departed through the front of the house. His gang of hardcases was lolling about in the bunkhouse when he burst in.

'You boys git ready to ride. Green, you hightail it to town. Git hold of Grant or Austin. Tell them I got news of Harry Grant. From what I can gather he's out of prison but hurt bad. He's holed up somewhere. We're gonna find out where.'

Bagot set out with his men into Lourdes. He left one man with instructions to follow the young stranger.

'If'n he rides anywhere other than Lourdes, you hightail it into town and inform me pronto.'

Richard Grant was out of town on business. Bagot found David Austin and informed him of his findings.

'Son of a bitch, if'n Harry comes back it'll

queer everythin'. Jeez, Cousin Richard *would* have to be missin' at a time like this.' Austin bit his lip nervously. 'Spread your men around town. Keep an eye out for that kid. My guess is that that Injun'll send him straight to Harry's Aunt Dorothy. Have her house staked out. I want to know everyone who comes and goes there.'

A few hours later a well-laden buggy left Lourdes. Todd Bagot swore when he saw the old Indian ride out alongside the vehicle.

'Gawdamn treacherous Injun, when this is finished he won't have no job at the Big G. He won't have no hide left neither. I'll take a bull-whip to him.'

David Austin paced up and down as he was told the latest developments.

'Gawdamn! Gawdamn! Gawdamn! There's no way we can allow Harry Grant to come back to the Big G. That's what Richard is doin' now. He's puttin' his lawyers to disinherit Harry Grant. We dug up some old law about a felon not being fit to take possession of property. We reckoned by the time Harry Grant comes out of prison we'll have everythin' in place. If'n he's 'lowed to come back now it's all straw in the wind.'

Bagot watched David Austin. He hid his contempt for the man. Richard Grant was a man of action and instant decisions. This man was a dithering fool. Anyone with an iota of common sense knew what had to be done. This Harry Grant fella had to be stopped. There was only one way to do that. Bagot tapped the butt of his revolver. He knew just what would stop him. But he waited for David Austin to come to the same conclusion.

'You'll have to follow the buggy. You say two women went in it. That would be old Dorothy, an' I don't know the younger one.' David Austin was sweating with the pressure of the decisions being forced on him. 'Somehow you'll have to stop Harry Grant.' He couldn't bring himself to say what he expected of the gunman. 'Just use your discretion...'

Bagot smiled grimly. He motioned to his second in command. Mott Green tapped his gun butt in response. The two gunfighters sauntered out of the Hot Spur.

In a short time a group of gunmen could be seen heading out of Lourdes. David Austin had just released the hounds of hell. As far as they were concerned Harry Grant would not be coming home to claim his inheritance.

22

Harry Grant floated up and up. He felt as though he was existing in some sort of dream. Though the dream was more a nightmare of pain. At last he drifted to the surface and began to take note of his surroundings. It was broad daylight outside yet the shades were drawn.

The room was decidedly feminine. Elegant curtains covered the chintz drapes. On the large oak dresser lace mats were used to protect the wood against accidental damage. Arranged about the place were flower-vases and ornaments. The flowers gave off a delicate scent that added to the dainty sense of femininity.

Harry became aware there was someone else in the darkened bedroom. By the bedside was a cane-armchair. He could make out someone reclining in the chair. The person had long hair and wore a dress. For a while he studied the woman. She was very quiet. He could just hear her peaceful breathing. That much established, he tried to figure out where he was.

He shifted into a more comfortable position and a large bird of prey raked vicious talons across his back. Harry arched in the bed as pain and memory flooded through him.

The door opened and someone glided into the room. The woman beside the bed remained slumped in the chair. A cool hand slid on to his brow. Harry stayed still. He couldn't figure out who all these women were. Surely this couldn't be the county hospital?

'Allison, Allison.' The name was whispered. Harry tensed. Allison! He only knew one Allison. Then he relaxed. Coincidence. There was bound to be more than one woman named Allison in the world. The seated figure stirred.

'Dorothy. I ... I'm sorry. I must have dozed off.'

'And any wonder. You've had no sleep for two days now. Go and put your head down. I'll watch now.'

The whispers continued. Harry thought furiously.

'Dorothy ... is that you, Aunt Dorothy?' His voice was the croak of a rusty hand-pump.

'Harry, oh Harry. Thank God. Oh Harry, we were so worried...

A figure moved to the window and the drapes were drawn. Bright sunlight flooded into the room. Harry gaped at the woman by the bed.

'Miss Allison? Is that really you? How did you git here? And even so, how did I git here? What happened? Where am I?' Harry's bewilderment was evident in his disjointed questioning.

'There, there now, son. Don't get excited. You're in good hands. Allison here has not left your side since we got here.'

Harry lay pondering this strange turn of events – Miss Allison and his Aunt Dorothy caring for him.

'Luke, what about Luke? I ... I did my best, Miss Allison...'

'Luke's fine. He's here with us. Can't you remember?'

Harry fell silent. He could remember and the memories were bad – the stuff of nightmares. By the state of his body it had been all that and more. But the two women refused to answer any more questions till he had taken a little food and drink.

However, more surprises were in store.

'Son of a gun, Harry Grant. You always

was a lucky son of a bitch. If'n you fell in a barrel of buffalo-chips you'd come out smelling of rotgut whiskey.'

Harry stared as his old friend Ben North walked into the room. Crowding in behind him came Luke Parsons, grinning like an ape with a bad case of wind. Behind him again came a familiar old face like a waxed walnut – nodding hard enough to loosen it from its moorings. The bedroom got a little crowded. It was almost too much for Harry.

'Harry Grant, if'n you don't close your mouth, that vase of flowers'll fall in it.'

Aunt Dorothy tried to shoo them all out of the bedroom again but no one wanted to leave now that Harry was awake. But Dorothy was a formidable dowager. Harry lay back and smiled as his aunt cleared the protesting men. At last only Allison and herself remained.

'Allison, you look done in. I want you to go next door and get some sleep.'

Dorothy had physically to escort Allison to the door of an adjoining bedroom.

'I'll be only next door if you need me.' Harry smiled at her, thinking he did not want her to go. Her gaze lingered on him then she slipped through the door and was gone.

'That girl must be done in. She hasn't left your side since we got here.'

'I got you and her to thank, I guess. What about Pa?'

Even before she replied he knew by her shocked face that something was terribly amiss.

'You don't know!' she whispered. 'Oh, Harry, I ... I thought the prison authorities would have informed you... Big John's gone ... last week ... he ... I...' she trailed off, gazing at him with stricken eyes.

Harry squeezed shut his own eyes. *Don't cry, son,* Big John would tell him when he came running after a childish mishap. *Men don't cry.* And Harry had learned not to cry. Now, as he felt the sharp pangs of grief, the prick of tears under his eyelids threatened to unman him. Even after all he had endured this was the cruellest blow of all. Big John Grant – solid, dependable – laid low by the bullet of a drifter. The cruellest blow. He felt the bed shift as his aunt sat. Her hands gripped his.

'I'm so sorry, Harry. It never occurred to me. I ... I ... you've lost a father. I've lost a brother.'

They sat in silence. Somehow her presence helped soothe his grief.

'Rest now, Harry. Sleep and rest are the best medicine at the moment.'

She drew the curtains again and tiptoed from the room. Harry lay on his side, trying to ease the pain of his back. The pain in his mind was not so easily relieved. In spite of these discomforts he dozed on and off. It was some time later that a commotion downstairs roused him somewhat. Voices were raised and he strained to make sense of the noises. At one stage he thought he heard someone call out his name.

Harry struggled into an upright position in the bed. Shards of pain tore at the scabs beginning to form on his lacerated back. The sounds were muffled and indistinct. He contemplated getting out of bed. Throwing back the covers took most of his strength. Before he could swing his legs on to the floor he heard heavy footsteps on the stairs. The door of the bedroom burst open. Harry Grant stared at the tough-looking man framed in the doorway. He held a Colt in his big hand and he looked as if he knew how to use it.

23

'Well, well, well, I think I've cornered me a ring-tailed bobcat.'

Harry stared at the big man as he stepped inside. The Colt was pointed straight at Harry.

'What the hell's goin' on? Who are you?'

'Me? Bagot's the name but it doesn't matter a darn who I am. I guess you're this'n here Harry Grant that's givin' certain parties sleepless nights.'

The man moved to the bottom of the bed. Harry stared up at the Colt now pointing directly at his face. It looked as big as a cannon.

'Harry Grant, you've caused enough trouble. I'm here to see it stops right now.'

'What the hell you talkin' about?' A sudden thought struck him. 'Where are my friends? What have you done with them?'

'I can see why you're a trouble maker. You ask too many damned questions.' The stranger grinned sourly. 'Your friends is all sittin' nice and quiet in the parlour. My friends is sittin' with them makin' sure they cause no trouble. Mind you, had to club one of them – a feisty young fella with a moustache. Claimed he was a marshal or somethin'. Whatever, he's a marshal with a sore head now.'

'Damn you to hell! What's this all about anyway? I never done nothing to you. Someone's hirin' you to do this. You aimin' to shoot me?'

That surly grin came again.

'Sure as hell am.' The big gun was cocked – the sound loud and startling in the bedroom. Harry stared steadily at the gunman.

'This makes no sense. I just got outta prison. I'm mendin' from a floggin'. I ain't in no fit state to cause you no trouble.'

'You see, that's the sort of fella you are. You musta done somethin' to be flogged for. I can see for myself you're a troublesome sorta fella.'

'Look, I got money, land, cattle. I just learned my old man died and left me a large ranch. I can make you a better offer than the folk that're hirin' you to kill me. Name your price.'

Harry had no intention of paying the man anything. He was just stalling, hoping something would happen to his advantage.

Though he could not see how he could come off the bed and grab the gun before it went off. The man holding the gun looked more than capable of using it.

He realized the whole thing had been well planned. Ben and Luke had been surprised and overpowered. Now this hired killer seemed to relish his hold over Harry. Harry knew the man was toying with him. As a cat played with a captured mouse or bird before the kill, so the gunman toyed with him.

'The price?' Bagot smiled that obnoxious smile. There was the coldness of death in his eyes. Harry knew he had to make a move soon. He knew his chances of overpowering the killer were next to zero. But he had to make the effort.

He was not the type to go meekly to the slaughter. The killer wanted him to have a go. Killing a helpless man in bed would not be so much fun. Like the cat, the death was not important. What were important were the struggles of the prey to survive. So the gunman taunted his victim and his victim waited and talked and cast about for a chance to fight back.

Neither of the antagonists noticed the door of the adjoining room move ever so slightly. Slowly the aperture widened. If

Bagot had looked he would have seen, in the gloomy shadows, a pale face peering out through the narrow gap. But he did not look. He was becoming bored. It was time for action.

Bagot reached into the bed and gathered the quilt in his big hand. He began to fold the thick material round his gun hand effectively covering over the weapon.

'If'n you pray, I'd start now,' he said. 'The quilt muffles the shot,' he explained. 'Don't want to attract any unnecessary attention.'

'I ... uh ... need to kneel by the bed.' Harry began to move.

'No you don't! Just stay right there.'

'At least let me kneel,' Harry pleaded drawing his legs underneath his body.

'Go to hell!' Bagot snarled. He straightened his arm and the rolled-up quilt was about four feet from Harry's face. The shot rang out as Harry launched himself in a hopeless attempt to beat the bullet from Bagot's gun.

It seemed strange, Harry thought, as he scrabbled desperately across the bed to get to the gunman – it seemed strange that he couldn't feel the bullet. The crack of the shot was odd too. It didn't seem to come from the bundled-up gun. Harry put that down to the muffling effects of the quilt. These thoughts flashed through his mind as he launched himself over the end rail.

The gunman was staggering sideways, an anguished look on his face. Blood poured from a hole in the side of his face. He opened his mouth to cry out and blood spurted out and on to the front of his shirt.

Harry cannoned into the quilt pod, pushing it hard against the retreating gunman. His attack threw Bagot off balance. They crashed to the floor with Harry on top. Harry smashed his fist into the gunman's face.

He aimed the punch at the blood he could see on the man's cheek. Bagot screamed and wriggled desperately, trying to push Harry off. Harry head-butted. He scored on Bagot's nose. The gunman opened his mouth to yell and gagged as blood poured back down his throat. Bagot's eyes opened wide as he gasped for breath. Harry head-butted again.

Bagot fought back with mounting desperation. A situation that had seemed completely under his control had now deteriorated into a life or death struggle.

Bagot was on the floor with Harry on top and Harry was pounding away at the gunman's face. Blood was pouring from the mouth wound and running back down into Bagot's throat. Harry's head-butt had smashed his nose. The gunman was drowning in his own blood.

For Bagot it seemed his only hope was to get his gun turned around and to blast this stubborn cowboy to hell. His legs threshed around on the floor, his heels scoring marks on the wooden boards. Desperately he pulled the trigger. The explosion was startling in the closeness of the men's bodies. Harry felt the hot blast as the bullet emerged from the quilt, narrowly missing his face. Flames burst from the material.

The smoke from the burning quilt spiralled into Harry's eyes and nose. Now it was his turn to gasp for air.

He shook his head vigorously in an attempt to clear the choking fumes. His legs straightened as he threshed about, trying desperately to avoid the choking fumes. He felt the end of the bed against his bare feet. Desperately he thrust hard as he tried to push up and away from the fumes. He rode high above the lethal bundle trapped between him and his assailant and the package rolled with him. At that fatal moment the gun went off again.

Harry was deafened by the second report. Blood splattered his face and hair. He blinked in surprise, temporally blinded. Desperately he continued to hammer away at Bagot. He could feel the wet sogginess of the man's face as his fist battered home. Bagot did not fight back. And then he heard someone calling his name.

'Mr Grant, please Mr Grant, please...'

He blinked in surprise. The man underneath him had ceased struggling. Harry looked into the face only there was no face. Where the face should have been was instead a piece of raw and bloody meat.

24

'Mr Grant, please Mr Grant, are you all right?'

Harry turned away from the horror that had been the face of Bagot before the bullet had ploughed through it. Another face swam out of the fog of blood and smoke – the white, anxious face of a young girl.

'Miss Allison,' he croaked. He was not to know that his own face was splattered with gore from the man lying beneath him. The shot from Bagot's gun had entered under the killer's chin and emerged through the forehead, spraying blood on to Harry. 'You ... you ... OK?'

'Yes. Oh, Mr Grant, are you hurt bad?'

Harry could have replied that he hurt from the ends of his fingers to the tips of his toes but at that moment someone called from downstairs.

'Todd ... Todd, what's happening up there?'

He rolled off the dead man and saw the small, snub-nosed derringer still gripped in

Allison's hand. For the first time he realized what had happened – why Bagot had not shot him – why the shot from the muffled gun had not blasted him. The shot hadn't come from Bagot's gun. The shot had come from the small gun in Allison's hand.

The small-bore bullet had struck the killer in the side of the face and thrown him off balance, effectively saving Harry's life. He had no time to think further on this. Footsteps could be heard on the stairs and the voice was calling again for Bagot.

Harry shouted out: 'All right, all right...' in the hope of stalling the man.

He tugged at the quilt. The dead gunman still clutched the Colt that had ended his own life. Frantically Harry prised the gun loose. On all fours he crawled to the door. Turning to Allison, he signalled for her to open the door. She reached across and wrenched it open.

Harry stared out into the landing. A head was almost level with his but the eyes were focused above Harry. The man was obviously expecting to see Bagot's tall form. Instead he saw someone crouched on the floor. It took a moment for him to register that something was amiss. In that fatal moment Harry fired the Colt. He had seen enough to realize that the man was a stranger. Aware of the ruthless nature of the men Bagot was likely to have as sidekicks he took no chances but shot to kill.

The man didn't have a chance to call out. The heavy-calibre bullet smashed into the bridge of his nose. He arched back without a sound and somersaulted back down the stairs. Gun thrust out before him, Harry crawled to the head of the stairs in time to see the man crash to the bottom and lie unmoving. He heard shouted curses.

'What the hell's goin' on?' someone shouted. 'Jeez, Green's dead. Lying out there in the hall. Where the hell's Bagot?'

Harry did not answer. He lay on the landing, peering down at the sprawled figure of Green. There was a movement behind him.

'Stay in the bedroom,' he hissed without turning round.

'Bagot, where the hell are you?'

Harry trained the gun on the doorway to the parlour. Bagot had said his friends were being held there. That was where the attackers would emerge.

The gun felt heavy in his hand. He could feel a wetness on his back. His lacerations had broken open and were weeping blood. Dull pain throbbed in every part of his body. Waves of sickness threatened to overwhelm him. He wanted to do nothing but crawl back into the bed and pull the covers up over him and sleep for a month. But his friends were downstairs, held hostage by desperadoes.

Two members of the gang were dead. That might be enough to spook them, and then again they might risk a gun-battle to exact revenge. Harry blinked to clear the sweat and blood from his stinging eyes. He tried to focus on the parlour door. His vision swam and small dots spiralled across his sight like flocks of crows following a plough.

There was more shouting and something crashed in one of the rooms. Harry wished he were strong enough to rush down the stairs. He knew that if he tried to stand he would probably pitch down the steps just as Green had.

The gun in his hand felt as heavy as an ancient muzzle-loader. Then a shadow spread out from the parlour door across the polished floor of the hallway.

Harry tensed. His finger tightened on the trigger. The gun wavered as his vision swam. Come out quickly, he prayed, before I let this gun fall down the stairs. A head poked out and Harry fired.

The shot smashed a flower-vase on the hall-stand. Coloured bits of ceramic scattered into the floor. Water splashed over the stand and dripped to the floor. The head disappeared.

'Gawdamn it to hell, is that you, Harry?'

Harry blinked. His eyes burned in his head. He blinked some more as he tried to ease them.

'Ben, Ben, it's me, Harry. What's happenin'?'

'I'll tell you what's happenin', you damned near shot my blasted head off. Now back up. Those mavericks have gone. They scarpered when their boss took a death leap from the top of the stairs. I take it that was your doin'?'

'It's all right, Ben. Come on up.'

Harry let his head droop to the floor. The hand holding the Colt rested on the top step of the stairs. A soft touch on his arm drew his gaze to the girl at his side.

'Miss Allison,' he whispered, 'you saved my life.'

She took his hand and soft tears rained down on to him. He gazed in wonder at the vision kneeling beside him.

'Don't cry, Miss Allison. It's over. You're safe now.'

Then strong hands were helping him into the bedroom with Allison fussing by his side. Luke came pounding up the stairs, closely followed by Moss.

'Mr Harry, you mighty fighter even when sick,' the old Indian announced proudly.

'You're gawdamn right he is. He gawdamn near as killed me along with these gunhawks,' grumbled the marshal. Harry smiled at the evident relief in his old friend's voice.

Bagot's body was dragged downstairs. Harry heard the voices in the hallway. As he drifted in and out of sleep he couldn't understand why Allison held tightly to his hand. It gave him a good feeling, then he remembered Luke and some of the goodness dissipated.

Some day they'll go their own way again, he thought regretfully. But it was exceptionally good to lie there and feel her soft presence. Somehow it seemed to ease the terrible aching in his body. The aching in his heart was another matter altogether.

'Harry, someone to see you.'

Harry's day-dreaming was suddenly interrupted. Ben North motioned to someone out on the landing. A portly, balding man stepped inside the room. On his chest was a silver star. Harry blinked. Were the prison gates beckoning again?

'Harry, this is Sheriff Pearson, he's here about the fracas.'

Before Harry could reply a female voice spoke up.

'Sheriff, you've got the wrong person. It wasn't Mr Grant who shot those men. It was me.'

The three men in the room gaped at Allison. She stood defiantly by the bedside, her hands clenched into fists as if she were about to fight for Harry Grant's guilt or innocence.

'Well, miss, I sure appreciate your honesty, but...'

Allison took a step forward and held out her hands.

'I tell you I'm the one you want. You can arrest me. I shot that man Bagot. Mr Grant is innocent.'

'Miss ... I come here...'

'Goddamn it, Sheriff, I did it! Here's the gun.' Allison produced the small derringer.

Allison's attempt at swearing, along with the passion she exhibited as she attempted to shield Harry from the law was too much for Ben North. He snorted as he tried to disguise his laughter. Sheriff Pearson gave him a pained look.

'Miss, if you'll just back up a moment an' let me explain...'

Harry just stared at Allison. This was a side of her he could not have imagined. She stood straight as a ramrod – a bulwark between him and the lawmen. What a woman, he thought. I wouldn't want to get on the wrong side of her. She reminded him of a wildcat he had cornered once.

The cat had stood much like this young girl stood now – back arched, defying him to come any closer. He had wondered why she did not flee. Just as he lined her up in the sights of his rifle the soft mewling had reached his ears.

'Gawddamn it, young 'uns.'

He had slowly backed up. To this day he wondered why he had not shot the cat and disposed of the kittens. Watching Allison defy the lawman he knew why he had left the cat to her family.

Just a moment ago he had made the attempt to rescue his friends. His own safety had had no bearing on the undertaking. Now he could only marvel at the unwavering courage of Allison as she tried to protect him. His throat choked as he stared at the young woman.

Allison still held out her slim, white wrists

to the lawman.

'You can cuff me if you want, Sheriff. I'll come quiet.'

'Gawddamn it girl, will you back off an' let a man git a word in?' the sheriff burst out. 'I ain't arrestin' no one.' The sheriff's face was bright red as he spoke. 'Beggin' your pardin for swearin, ma'am.'

Allison blinked and her eyes opened wide. She opened her mouth but no sound came. Before she could utter, the sheriff hurriedly went on.

'We apprehended some of those rannies afore they could ride out. We got them talkin'. They was tryin' to save their own skin. They told us Green and Bagot had brung 'em along for the ride. Said as they didn't hold with no killin'. Sure as hell don't believe 'em. They told us Green and Bagot was sent along by a David Austin for to git rid of Harry Grant. I ain't arrestin' no one. So if'n you'll just stop showin' your wrists off 'nless you wanna spend a night in the cells. Sure would be mighty pleased to hold a fine young filly like yourself in my jail.'

Harry watched as Allison's face went from pale defiance to crimson embarrassment. If Ben North's grin had got any wider the top of his head would have become unstable.

Allison's hands flew to her mouth. Slowly she reversed away till the back of her knees hit the bed and she fell backwards. Harry grunted as she landed on top of him. She half-turned and suddenly she and Harry were face to face.

Harry stared into limpid green eyes and was instantly lost. His aches and pains and fatigue faded and for a moment he forgot all else, only the nearness of this red-haired goddess. The room faded. Harry was aware of someone talking but the words made no sense. Then Allison gave a little gasp and struggled to get up again. The spell broke and Harry was again in a world of pain and uncertainty.

25

'Harry, this is madness. You ain't in no fit state to go traipsin' off like this.'

Harry Grant stood by the buggy looking at his friend Ben North. He held on to the side of the carriage and waited for the dizzy spell to pass.

'Ben, you know this thing has to be ended. Aunt Dorothy told it straight all along. Richard Grant is the cause of all my troubles. Only I hadn't the brains to see it. We all thought she was a daft old woman rantin' in grief over the death of her husband, Uncle Tom. I gotta do this. No one else can. It's my responsibility. My family honour is at stake. We reared ourselves a rat. I gotta stop that rat from causin' any more trouble.'

At that moment Moss appeared. The old Indian carried an ancient shotgun. Without saying a word he placed the weapon in the carriage and climbed into the driver's seat.

'Moss, what'n hell you think yore doin'?'

The Indian stared impassively at Harry. Broad stripes of paint criss-crossed his face.

'Master Harry go to war. Moss go to war.' The old man turned his face resolutely forward. Harry opened his mouth to remonstrate but something about the set of the old servant stopped him.

'Gawddamm it,' he muttered shaking his head. The waves of dizziness returned. He gripped hard on the wood of the carriage. From behind the building a rider appeared leading a saddle-horse. Harry stared in disbelief as the youth pulled up beside the buggy. The young man grinned at him, then turned to Ben North and held up the reins of the horse he was leading.

'Saddled up for you, Mr North.'

'No, no ... I ain't 'lowin' this. No way. Git down of'n that horse, Luke Parsons. This ain't nothin' to do with you.' He turned back to the lawman. 'Nor you, Ben North. What the hell...!'

Ben North grinned at his friend and slapped him on the back. Harry almost screamed as the hand landed on his still-tender flesh. The pain took his breath away. He could make no more protest as the lawman took the reins from Luke and swung easily into the saddle. Before he could rally to discourage his friends from coming on this journey two women came out of the house on to the boardwalk.

Aunt Dorothy walked over and gently embraced him.

'I know better'n try to dissuade you from this foolish venture, Harry. You're a Grant. I only wish you were in better shape.'

Harry looked over her shoulder at the young girl waiting to say her farewells. Tears were spilling unrestrained down her cheeks.

'Miss Allison ... I ... er... I didn't ask Luke...'

Harry stumbled to a stop. The tears were unmanning him. He wanted to weep himself. Big John's words came back. *Men don't cry, son.*

'Goddamn you, Harry Grant, if'n you ain't the blind'nist man I ever met.'

Harry stared at his aunt. In all his life he had never heard his aunt swear.

'Aunt Dorothy...!'

'Goddamn it Harry,' she repeated. 'If'n you don't take this gal and kiss before you ride off on this foolish venture I ... I ... I'm gonna kick your butt.'

Harry stared in bewilderment at his aunt. He was afraid to look at Allison.

'Goddamn kids!'

Aunt Dorothy grabbed Allison. Without ceremony she turned and thrust the girl up against Harry. If the carriage hadn't been there Harry would have fallen back into the road.

'Oh, Harry!'

A pair of soft arms wound around his neck. Soft lips crushed against his mouth. Harry's head spun. At last they came up for air. Harry stared into those green eyes. The tears were still spilling down the soft cheeks. He reached out a finger and touched the wetness. This made no sense but he did not protest.

'She loves you, you big lummox. Cain't you see that.' His aunt was relentless. 'For God's sake say somethin'.'

Harry opened his mouth. 'I...'

'Its all right, Harry ... you needn't say anythin'...'

'But Luke, I thought you and Luke ... he ... you...'

The green eyes gazed into his.

'What about Luke?'

'I thought you an' he ... I thought you an' he was betrothed.'

Then Allison was hugging him and his back was hurting like hell but he did not object.

'Luke's my brother ... my twin. Oh, Harry, and all this time you thought ... you didn't

190

know.' She was laughing and crying at the same time.

It took some time to disentangle the pair. Neither seemed willing to let go of the other. At last Harry prised himself away from this wonderfully fragrant girl. Trying not to appear like a crippled old man he clambered up beside Moss.

He had borrowed Aunt Dorothy's carriage, for he did not think he would be fit for the long haul to Lourdes on the back of a horse. The old Indian flicked the reins. The buggy lurched forward.

'I'll come back, Allison. Don't you worry none. You an' me got some catchin' up to do.'

Harry braced himself against the seat. He tried not to lean on the backrest. Despite his assurances to Allison and Dorothy his back still felt as if it were on fire. It was going to be a test of his mental and physical resources just to get to Lourdes, never mind brace his cousin and whatever gunslingers he had gathered round him. Then a vision of soft green eyes swam into his mind.

'I will come back for you, Allison.'

26

There was a swarm of black ants teeming across his back, each one armed with red-hot needles for pincers. Harry almost fell out of the buggy when he tried to alight. Pretending to review his surroundings he held on to the side of the carriage as he waited for the agony to subside. Moss clambered down and tied the reins to a post.

'Remember, Moss, you do nothin' till you hear shootin'. Then you come in like a cougar.'

The old man grinned. He had translated his native name once. The rough interpretation came out as Moves like a Cat. During his service in the Grant household he had become Moss. Master Harry was the chief now. Moss would follow the young warrior into hell.

On the outskirts of town the little party had split up. Harry had no doubt that Richard Grant would know he was coming. Some of the men sent out with Bagot and Green had escaped. They would have ridden post-haste to Lourdes and alerted his cousin. Not knowing what was in store for their reception they had to improvise.

Luke was to ride up to the Hot Spur and disembark for a drink. He was not known to anyone and was to move among the tables and join a card-game or just sit drinking. His task was to watch Harry's back. Marshal North was to circle around to the back of the street and force an entry into the rear of the saloon. Harry would leave Moss outside as back-up.

Harry braced himself before he pushed through the doors of the Hot Spur. He touched the butt of the big Colt he had taken from Bagot. It was tucked into the waistband of his trousers. It was all that stood between him and Richard Grant's gunnies.

'Redeye,' he instructed the barman. The man didn't seem to know him or if he did he didn't let on. He set a tumbler and a bottle on the bar. Harry poured and downed the drink in one gulp. The fiery liquor hit his throat and burned a rivulet down into his gullet. Harry gasped and poured another. The fire in his veins spread.

He wanted to finish his drink, stride out of the Hot Spur and ride back to Allison.

'Hello Harry, good to see you.'

Harry turned and stared into the pale, sweating face of David Austin. Harry's eyes went cold as he contemplated his cousin.

'I was sorry about Big John. We all miss him. Bad business that. Good to see you out of prison again, Harry. I couldn't believe they sent you away for that. We was doin' our best for to git you off.'

David Austin was babbling nervously. He took out a kerchief and dabbed at his face.

'Where's Cousin Richard, David? He send you to do his dirty work?'

'What, Harry...? Oh, Richard. He should be along sometime. Usually pops in later.'

David Austin ran a finger inside his collar as if it was suddenly too tight.

'He's here David, isn't he. Right now he's watching us through some peephole. You're to distract me while his hired gunmen git in position.'

Harry suddenly gripped the sweating man by the coat and spun him round. The Colt was in his hand. He jammed the barrel into the trembling David Austin's ear.

'Just point to where he's at. I want him to know I know what he's up to.'

'Harry ... Harry, this is all wrong. I don't know what you're thinkin'. No one's gonna harm you. You got it all wrong.'

Harry began to spot them then, dotted here and there amongst the card-players and drinkers. Hard eyes were watching him. Predators were ready to pounce. He turned the gun and pulled the trigger. A big full mirror behind the bar exploded as the bullet smashed into the glass. In the silence that followed his sudden action Harry began to speak.

'Anyone makes a move agin me and I put a bullet in Austin's brain.' He could feel David Austin trembling in his grasp. 'For those who don't know me, I'm Harry Grant. My pa was Big John Grant. He was shot here in the Hot Spur and died later. I killed the man that shot him. The man I shot was a hired killer. My belief is that my cousin, Richard Grant hired him. Now I've come for my cousin. This family feud has to finish now before any more of my family are murdered. I'm callin' you out, cousin. Come out from whatever rat-hole you're hidin' in.'

Men sat or stood around the Hot Spur un-moving. In the silence after Harry's speech someone coughed, but no one stirred. Every one waited.

Harry watched the hired killers. His move had wrong-footed them. They were awaiting instructions from the man who had hired them. He spotted Luke sitting at one of the tables. A collective gasp went up as the bat-wings banged open and Moss came through. Then all hell broke loose.

The ancient shotgun went off with a report like thunder. The shot passed close to Harry. Behind him the barman cried out and his scattergun clattered on to the bar top. Richard Grant's hired gunmen went for their irons. David Austin sagged at the knees. Harry could not hold him; he had to let the man go and Austin fell to the sawdust floor. Harry thumbed off a shot at the closest gunman. Not waiting to see the effect of his bullet he threw himself on to the bar top and rolled over to fall behind its cover. He almost screamed as agony seared through his body.

Shards of mirror showered around him as he tried to lever himself upright. The noise of gunfire in the bar was fierce. Bullets hammered in and around Harry's position. In a lull Harry took a quick look over the top. Seeing a man with his gun out he fired off a round. The gunman spun round and dropped. Bullets again hammered into the wall behind him.

Harry crawled past the bloodied corpse of

the barman towards the end of the bar. As he peered round the wooden planking he spied a man on the stairs blazing away in his direction. Again he shot. He had the satisfaction of seeing the man tumble back over the rails.

He had no idea how his comrades were faring. As if in answer to the thought he heard the boom of Moss's ancient weapon. He risked another quick look into the saloon. Splinters of wood stung his face as a bullet ploughed into the bar. Harry cursed and pondered his next move. He was forestalled before he could figure out how he could break this stalemate.

'Cease firin', damn it. Hold it, damn it!'

The firing petered out. After the racket the silence seemed oppressive. Harry lay in a wreckage of glass. He didn't recognize the voice.

'Harry Grant, this is Sheriff Garrison here. You're all finished up. Two of your men are down. We got the other one here with a gun at his head.'

'How do I know you're not lyin', Sheriff. You've lied to me before. I got a prison sentence outta that.'

'Harry, Harry, Harry.' This time someone else spoke. He recognized the tones of his cousin, Richard Grant – the cause of all his problems. 'I guarantee no one will shoot. Just have a look. You're all washed up.'

Harry thought for a while. If he shouted out a name it might betray one of his friends. Then again, he was trapped behind the bar. At some stage he would have to come out.

'All right, I'm standin' up. But I still got my gun. Don't mess me about or I'll start shootin' again.'

Not wanting to emerge where they were expecting him he crawled behind the bar. It wasn't easy, for the floor was littered with shards of glass. At last he stood up slowly.

The first thing he noticed was Luke. A gunman was holding one arm around the youth's neck. In his other hand he pressed a gun against Luke's head.

He couldn't see Richard Grant. Sheriff Garrison stood near the door. Beside him on the floor lay Moss, his shotgun lying beside him. Then he saw Ben.

The marshal was propped up against a wall holding a hand to a shoulder. Blood leaked through his fingers. He looked up wryly at Harry and gave a crooked grin.

'Sorry, pardner, I guess I messed up.'

As Ben spoke Harry saw Richard Grant

standing near the wounded man. He held a pistol pointed at the lawman. He smiled across at Harry.

'Well, Harry, do you want to go on fightin'? Your two pardners will die first. After that I doubt if'n you'll survive, either.'

Harry's eyes flicked around the saloon. Most of the customers were lying on the floor where they had thrown themselves when the gunfight began. He noticed a couple of dead gunnies sprawled in the sawdust.

'How do you want to end this?' he asked at last.

'Now you're talkin' sense. Throw out your weapon. Then these rannies can go free. When they're out of the way we settle this. Just you an' me.' Richard displayed his most charming smile. 'Winner take all.'

'Don't trust him, Harry,' gritted Ben. 'He's a liar and a killer. You'd as well trust a rattlesnake.'

'I know, Ben. But I got no other hand to play.' Harry looked at his cousin. His shoulders drooped despondently. 'You win, Richard. But I ain't givin' up my gun completely. I'll lay it on the counter here and step back while my friends go free. Like he says, I'd as well trust a rattlesnake.'

'OK, Harry boy. That's good enough.'

Harry laid his Colt on the bar top and stepped back. He watched dully as the sheriff instructed some men to carry Ben North out from the Hot Spur. His aunt had been right when she told him this was a foolish venture.

'Take him across to Doc Fleming,' Richard called out. 'Tell him to charge the treatment to me.'

Luke too was escorted from the saloon. He looked thoroughly subdued as two deputies escorted him outside.

'What about the Injun?' Harry asked.

'Don't worry about that piece of trash,' Sheriff Garrison replied with a grimace. 'They'll sweep him out in the gutter. The dogs'll have a feast.'

Harry stared at the crumpled figure of the old man and a cold anger began to build. When Richard Grant spoke Harry kept his eyes lowered. He did not want the man to see the rage in his eyes.

'OK Harry, we'll take your gun now.'

Harry nodded at the Colt lying on the counter.

'Take it. As I said, you win – this time, anyhow.'

Richard Grant laughed. He motioned for Sheriff Garrison to fetch the weapon.

'Don't you move,' the sheriff instructed Harry. His own weapon was pointed at Harry as he moved to the bar. Harry's shoulders slumped as he stood behind the bar – the picture of dejection.

The sheriff approached the bar. His portly frame was partly shielding Harry from the guns in the saloon. As the sheriff groped for the Colt amid the debris of broken glass his own gun wavered. It was then that Harry Grant moved.

A long shard of glass plunged into the hand reaching for the gun. The wounded man staggered back and his gun went off. The bullet hit something behind Harry. Ignoring the sheriff Harry scooped up the Colt. He had taken everyone by surprise. Harry saw Richard Grant raise his gun. He took a quick pot-shot at his cousin. Richard spun round as the bullet hit home. The sheriff was cursing as he nursed his wounded hand. Harry turned his wrist a fraction and shot the man in the face. The big man crashed backwards on to the sawdust. Harry swept his gun around the saloon looking for more targets. Suddenly there was a forest of hands in the air.

The shooting of Richard Grant and Sheriff Garrison dispersed any bravado the hired guns might have had. They hadn't the guts to tangle with a man prepared to shoot down a lawman.

'Don't shoot. The boss is hit. We don't want any more. We quit.'

'Then git the hell out,' gritted Harry. He held his fire as half a dozen men scrambled for the door.

Slowly he came round the bar into the saloon. Richard Grant lay against a pillar, his face white.

'Damn you, Harry, I'm shot bad. Git me to Doc Fleming.'

Harry stood looking down at the man who had been the cause of so much trouble. Slowly he raised the Colt.

'You won't need a doctor where I'm gonna send you.'

'Harry, listen. I never wanted this to happen,' the wounded man gasped. 'You can have the Big G back. I was only lookin' after it for you while you was in prison. Its all yours. I'll compensate you for everything.'

'Can you bring back Big John?' Harry asked coldly. He cocked the Colt. The click was loud in the saloon.

'Harry, for Gawd's sake, that was a mistake. I never meant for that to happen.'

'Confess and I might let you live. You

hired that gunslinger fella to kill Big John and me.'

Richard Grant looked into his cousin's eyes and was mortally afraid.

'Yes,' he whispered.

'Louder, Richard.' Harry indicated the townsfolk crouching on the floor where they had remained while the shoot-out was taking place. 'I don't think these folk heard you.'

'I ... I hired Jones ... he was supposed to...'

Something touched Harry on the back of the neck – something cold and hard and round.

'Don't turn round, Harry.' The voice of David Austin dripped with menace. 'Just drop your gun and back up from Cousin Richard. Nice and slow-like.'

'You took your damn-blasted time,' rasped Richard Grant. 'Shoot this bastard an' git me over to Doc Fleming.'

'Don't do this, David,' Harry said. 'Didn't you just hear him confess to murder. He hired that Jones fella to murder my old man.'

'Well, you see, Harry, it was me that fetched Mr Jones to Lourdes. So, in a way, I'm as guilty as Richard. Goodbye Harry.'

The shot blasted out. Harry was punched

in the back and pitched forward on top of his wounded cousin. As he fell the Colt in his hand discharged. He heard Richard Grant cry out.

There was a terrible weight on his back. Harry groaned. This was how death felt. It was an intolerable weight pressing him down on the motionless body of his cousin. Then the weight disappeared.

'Boss Harry, what you like?'

He looked at the strained face of old Moss.

'We go to the happy hunting-ground now, Moss,' he said, feeling foolish even as he voiced the belief.

'No, Boss Harry. Not yet ready. Mebby 'nother day. We go git medicine. Then ride to Big G. Me git old job back.' He grinned at Harry. 'You look you need plenty good feedin'.'

The old man was grunting as he tried to get Harry to his feet. Harry was able to stand under his own steam. He stared at the body of David Austin lying beside him. Where the back of his head should have been was a mass of blood and pulp.

'Had to aim high. Didn't want hit Boss Harry,' Moss said by way of explanation. For the first time Harry looked at his old friend. Blood soaked the front of his shirt.

'You old varmint, you weren't daid. You was just playin' possum.'

There was a hurt look in the old man's eyes.

'Not possum, Boss Harry. Me cougar.'

And Harry Grant laughed. He put his arm round the old man's shoulders and walked out into the night, leaving behind the dead men sprawled in the sawdust of the Hot Spur Saloon.

The publishers hope that this book has given you enjoyable reading. Large Print Books are especially designed to be as easy to see and hold as possible. If you wish a complete list of our books please ask at your local library or write directly to:

Dales Large Print Books
Magna House, Long Preston,
Skipton, North Yorkshire.
BD23 4ND

This Large Print Book, for people
who cannot read normal print,
is published under the auspices of

THE ULVERSCROFT FOUNDATION

... we hope you have enjoyed this book.
Please think for a moment about those
who have worse eyesight than you ...
and are unable to even read or enjoy
Large Print without great difficulty.

You can help them by sending a
donation, large or small, to:

**The Ulverscroft Foundation,
1, The Green, Bradgate Road,
Anstey, Leicestershire, LE7 7FU,
England.**
or request a copy of our brochure for
more details.

The Foundation will use all donations
to assist those people who are visually
impaired and need special attention
with medical research, diagnosis
and treatment.

Thank you very much for your help.